Winnipolago

By Julian Hamer

iv

Dedicated to Ellen, my beautiful wife and valiant editor.

Winnipolago

Tales from the Edge of Reason

By Julian Hamer

1.

Winnipolago properly deserves a formal introduction complete with longitude and latitude, geological origin and composition, flora and fauna such as it is, and an official census. But why spoil an otherwise perfectly sound narrative with facts? It is true that the reader may thereby mentally survey the terrain with an adequate comprehension of the particular context wherein these various impending adventures take place. But these accounts are neither geographical in nature nor are they supposed to offer a dry anthropological examination. If the reader wishes to know all about the rock formations and species of bird or rodent on Winnipolago there are many fine encyclopedias systematically compiled solely for that purpose. One merely has to search methodically under the letter *W*. However, that being said, the reader will enjoy this collection of tales just as considerably as if they were approached with complete ignorance. Furthermore, for the sake of the inhabitants, and through a profound respect for their privacy and various, albeit eccentric sensitivities, it would behoove the reader to take a small hop in faith and merely trust that Winnipolago most assuredly does exist, albeit merely in the minds of the extraordinary folk who reside there.

However, a general description will injure no one as long as the whereabouts remain sufficiently vague. But caution must remain our watchword. Heaven forbid that through a slip-of-the-tongue or by virtue of an overly zealous account, some foolhardy soul should feel inspired and determine to reconnoiter those distant shores, and become embroiled in an unpleasant misadventure. The miscellaneous countrymen whose fate it is to endure perpetual exile upon that bleakest, most hostile and insular expanse known to human kind, endure fools gladly but only those with whom they have established a working sufferance. The stranger, while pridefully well-meaning, benignly well-intentioned and naively artless, yet remains ill equipped if he or she imagines that those singular virtues will prepare and provide safe passage among the commonality that inhabits those northern isles.

But already I have neglected my own stern determination and spilled far too many beans so that the astute geographer or knowledgeable anthropologist may now attempt an educated stab and discover the whereabouts of that benighted country. Therefore, let no more be said by way of introduction and let the location and position of Winnipolago remain elusive lest, inadvertently, some adventurous spirit should stumble into such realms that persist between here and there in a refracted condition of uncertainty, far from the shores of reason. Let us, accordingly, begin at the beginning and introduce the reader to the disposition of the protagonists of Winnipolago. Firstly, we must begin, in all justice, with the weather and I will endeavor to detail, without exaggeration, the conditions of a perfect storm through the eye of the islander.

Winnipolagians suffer extremes of meteorological conditions. The day had started out pleasant enough, but the inhabitants recognized that something sinister was brewing. The sunrise had been a pitiable event while the gray green waves rose and swelled in a labor of ponderous bulk. The wind, at first no more than a zephyr, grew impatient and harsh. Suddenly, lightening cracked viciously like a whip across the leaden sky. The thunder rolled growling, and grumbling ominously as if determined not to be outdone, and appear any less menacing than the whitening blaze that blindingly floodlit the earth, one hilltop peak, one pasture and one boulder at a time. The sea heaved, surged and broiled, while the furious, foaming surf pounded the rocky shore, flinging high and smashing flotsam and jetsam with equal disregard, far up upon the ragged foreland. All the while the wind screamed with elemental passion like a harpy, whipping and thrashing the humiliated landscape with distracted derision. The heavens were gripped and torn, thrown at whim, hither and yon by the merciless violence of the storm.

The scrubby bushes that dotted the sparse island were plucked like chaff, thrashed, flailed and heedlessly castaway. Roofs, walls, entire homes were taken, tossed, scattered and callously discarded at the sport and caprice of the savage tumult. Lanes and roads became boiling, rivers sweeping, fervid, surging in mucky rapacity through the countryside, contemptuously devouring everything before and leaving only waste and squander in their wake.

The fury of the Gods was unleashed upon Winnipolago. Retribution gripped the tiny island and those sins that were thought forgotten swelled into stark recollection as collective apprehension of a final accounting gripped the island folk like an icy hand about the throat. Every soul was crumpled, prostrate, imploring the compassionate Omnipotent for clemency from each their own richly deserved purgatory.

But Millie was being philosophic.

The populace had gathered, a forlorn and wretched flock, within the only remaining sanctuary. The stone church alone, a deftly mortared, timeless barricade, buttressing massive timbers and mortared roof of native rock, sheltered the little congregation as a determined mother hen with all her chicks mustered, huddled beneath her enfolding wings.

The Preacher, who ordinarily boasted a hot-line with the Almighty, fell like the rest, although defiantly maintaining a semblance of authority, mumbling snatches of prayer, a holy verse or two, or suddenly a disorderly howl that was an aggregate of numerous fragments of hymn and canticle randomly assembled from an uncertain memory. He exhorted his little

3

assembly to repentance which, falling upon deaf ears, nevertheless fortified his courage because, after all, the sins of others appear far worse than our own and self-righteousness provides powerful balm to the uncertain soul. Finally, from the sanctuary of an upturned pew, he embarked upon a rambling sermon of shouted warnings that much resembled the tempest outside, softened only by limped platitudes when the wind suddenly hammered at the door and he retreated anxiously like a turtle beneath his pew, fearing that perhaps he had overstepped in his zeal.

Millie was blaming Mac.

It appeared that Mac had recently discovered something on the beach. A dead sailor had washed up just weeks before and Mac had retrieved the man's overcoat. It was wool, navy blue with a wide collar that turned up to shield the wearer from the wind. Mac had worn it with evident pride even though the original, rich color was compromised with patches of brine stain and it possessed a most unusual odor that was not at all pleasant. Added to his own unwashed condition, every one avoided Mac and his coat as if he had the bubonic plague and they were fearful that the smell was contagious.

Of itself, there was nothing unusual about taking possession of whatever Providence should choose to throw up on the beach even if the owner was still wearing it. Admittedly in this case, the owner was very, very dead and consequently, no one thought it improper that Mac should help himself. Upon any other island or civilized country, the authorities would remove the body and respectfully settle the necessary formalities before internment. The only authorities in Winnipolago, notwithstanding the Preacher, were the elements themselves and so the sailor was left where he was found until, eventually, the high tide took him to his final rest.

But it was not the coat that bothered Millie.

4

Mac had found a handsome pocketbook in the inside lining of the coat and began putting on airs, affecting the superior attitude of the highbrow, knowing full well that no one else in Winnipolago possessed anything as remotely plush and splendid as a calf-skin wallet with a tooled inscription in gold leaf. The absurdity was further compounded because the inscription was composed of the two capital letters: M and C. For Mac the next step was a very easy one and he effortlessly slipped into the persona of a seafaring man with his own and very personal credentials that he surreptitiously exposed to all who happened to glance his way.

He beheld himself as Mac, a naval gentleman with his monogram embossed in gold on the face of his personalized pocketbook, clear evidence of his superior rank and status, and plain proof of his distinction. He possessed conclusive verification, right there in his own hand, for all to see.

The best of minds behave strangely in exile and in situations of extreme privation. But Mac's intellect had always functioned uncertainly. Without a guiding hand to steer him, he had simply slipped a little further overboard than usual and was now perfectly content in this new role. He was a distinguished stranger who had suddenly appeared on the island and was endeavoring to make himself known with the decidedly strange, indigenous peoples who dwelt upon its rocky features.

The problem was that the stranger had discovered something inside the pocketbook and was eager to show this most esteemed possession to anyone willing enough to brave the combined odors of coat and Mac. One glance turned many a head in horror because Mac had found a family photograph and now claimed the two little children depicted there in black and white as his own. Fortunately, there was no picture of the wife of the unfortunate sailor or Mac would most certainly have become lost forever in some elaborate fiction of his own fabrication and, in his mottled mind, become not only parent, but husband and also family man.

The small vanity of the sea-soiled overcoat, the elegant pocketbook and the golden initials were of small consequence and would probably fade over time, restoring Mac to his former perplexed condition, and all would be forgiven and forgotten. Goodness knows Mac was hardly alone amongst the inhabitants of the island to stretch reality a little and, sometimes a lot, in order to discover its breaking strain. But adopting imaginary children did not bode well for the collective psyche of the other exiles. It seemed indecent somehow. Mac was showing the picture around with obvious pride and simultaneously drooling like a dog before a meal. He looked like a leering Polynesian effigy.

"Eh ee! Lookee, dees my kids. Mine own childer!"

Mac was not entirely hideous to behold, but he was severely encumbered by a slowness of wit and clumsiness of speech. This was remarkable in a human being because he appeared to contradict the Evolutionary Theory of Mr. Darwin by steadily acquiring simian characteristics without apparent notice or concern. It was not that his children were especially beautiful, but that Mac was very particularly dissimilar and it was the incongruity of resemblance between the youngsters and his own appearance and nature that upset Millie.

For Millie, it was Mac's obvious affection for the kids that proved to be the final straw. It was a blatant violence to her mothering instincts. No self-respecting woman of Millie's caliber, with even a speck of respect for maternal tradition, could possibly entertain Mac as the father of those two sweet fatherless babies. Resentment simmered within her soul and finally came to the boil.

"Mac! You take those darn things back down to the sea where you got them. You toss them out into the water and let them sink or drown as the good Lord sees fit. You ain't got no

6

right! And you ain't got no dignity! Get out o' here and give that poor dead man his rightful rest before you bring down a vengeance upon us all"

Millie was not really religious, but she was profoundly superstitious.

But Mac would not heed her because large words such as *dignity* and *vengeance* confused him and while he wrestled with their implication, he completely lost the gist of Millie's words. In any case, he was far too attached to his new identity, which added a further layer of confusion, so that, finally, he threw up his hands and resolutely stumped off.

But the storm set everything to rights. Several islanders, sprinting like frightened hares towards the safety of the church when the weather turned vengeful, heard Mac wailing from beneath the wreck of his cabin. The walls had fallen in all about him and the trash of ages sloshed about in the wreckage like a wildly bubbling, unsavory soup. Naval coat and wallet were nowhere to be seen and even if they could have been retrieved before the entire detritus was washed out to sea, the men were as sickened as Millie about Mac's imaginary family and determined to leave the furor of the storm to its own devices, and disposed of the wretched coat and its contents, once and for all.

Millie had wanted to abandon Mac to the cleansing power of the tempest and had he lost consciousness when the building fell upon him, and needed mouth-to-mouth resuscitation, there is every reason to believe that he would have been left to fend for himself or perish. But Mac was made of sterner stuff and scrambled to his feet, sobbing like a bereaved parent as he struggled with the rest of them through the pelting rain and gathering tumult towards high ground and the asylum of that rugged place of worship.

2.

Millie had met Mac, although somewhat indirectly, many years before their inadvertent arrival on Winnipolago. In those early days, Millie was a looker, and by all appearances, innocent and chaste. Men fell all over the place in love. Her daddy was a Montana rancher who had wanted a son, but Millie came into the world determined to be one hell of a woman in spite of his wishes to the contrary. She could do anything a cowboy could do but with such pronounced style and panache that eventually her father set his disappointment to one side and concluded that Millie was the son he had longed for after all, and he looked upon her thereafter as an honorary man.

Eventually, ranch life began to tire for her and when she was old enough, she took to the road with her trusty, trail worn saddle, hitching rides from one town to the next determined to make a name for herself as a cowgirl singer. Naturally, she had no trouble traversing that great Treasure State or those neighboring territories, and most travelers were more than willing to go out of their way to assist her in whatever manner they could.

Millie was only a very modest singer, but her act was full of expression from the neck downwards. Tone deaf, her voice sounded as if she yelled through a megaphone. But this description is not entirely fair. While her voice was raucous, the activity below was extremely compelling, and the patrons adored the depth and candor of her expression. For you see, Millie was an exceptional artiste and a little dissonance did not concern the audience one whit. They recognized intricacy and finesse when they saw it.

Millie had a generous figure in double measure and then some for goodwill. She was grateful for this blessing and considered it, if not money in the bank, at least collateral. Topped with a good pair of lungs essential to a Montana ranching girl,

Millie had the vernacular to go with it.

And that is where the trouble started.

A little one horse town named Hope in the middle of somewhere boasted a tavern called the Horny Toad. It was the kind of place frequented by roughs and toughs and peppered for good measure with down-and-outs. It was the only bar in town and Millie got herself a nice position singing to the patrons between dusk until dawn, drawing enthusiastic approval.

Millie's ranching background, droving, branding and breaking had left its mark and she would not suffer fools nor bad manners any more than she would allow a steer to kick her in the head. She considered disrespect akin to loafing and idleness and, maintaining strict principles concerning her own conduct, she had little tolerance for inconsiderate people. What riled her the most was that, while she made the considerable effort to dress herself prettily and polish up her act as best as she was capable so that the audience would feel that they were amply rewarded for their time and money, someone would talk or move, whisper, or order another drink while she was on-stage doing her darnedest.

Most of the boys behaved really well and retained respectful silence and rapt attention, albeit fearful that Millie, if offended, might leave the stage and refuse to return, perhaps for days. But, wouldn't you know, a stranger would loiter in now and again and upset Millie with his rudeness so that the entire audience would rise up as one man, eject the greenhorn culprit and plead sweetly with their starlet until she softened and returned, and all was forgiven. Even the penitent offender may be allowed back to her good graces with a suitable offering of flowers or some other symbol of contrition.

Not all transgressors left by the door. The saloon window, so frequently abused, was no longer glazed, but the horse trough beyond was kept expediently full at all times. Consequently, the offender might learn politeness through swift aerial transit, followed by sudden baptism, without the inconvenience of broken glass littering the bar, which might further upset Millie. Moreover, a good soaking was a fine sport that helped to relieve residual tension and ill-feeling.

Mac was fresh off the trail. His job was to cook for the cowboys, an employment that did not require exceptional verbal skills. His culinary proficiency was considered adequate to the task. As a tiny baby in a wicker basket, he was left on the doorstep of a hanging judge. The judge was appalled at the sight of the boy and left it to his Chippewa Indian cook to raise Mac in the kitchen, out of sight and mind. Thus, Mac learned to cook and was particularly adept at concocting imaginative preparations of rice, beans and, of course, elk and acorn pemmican. Thus, his future employment was assured.

Directly across the street from the Horny Toad was a soda fountain run by the Hope Temperance Society. It was strategically situated in order to inspire guilt among the clientele of the bar in the hopeful anticipation that some might forsake their drunken, wicked ways and opt for a carbonated beverage instead. Unfortunately, Mac had never developed a taste for anything but bourbon having been weaned from wet-nurse milk to water, then Jim Beam with water and, finally, Jim and nothing else.

Upon this one fateful day, that proved to be unlucky for him.

The Horny Toad was packed, wall-to-wall, standing room only. If you could find a patch of unoccupied floor, then you were lucky because Millie was on stage and all eyes were riveted, mouths agape and drooling, as that talented girl strutted through her act with mesmeric effect. Her audience was spellbound when all of a sudden a voice shattered the enchantment as Mac, after weeks on the trail stumbled through the crowd to the bar. With a thirst like a camel, he blurted out:

11

"Gee mee a boorbon ee!"

Horrified, the barman ducked out of sight as all eyes glared in unison upon the unfortunate. The piano music broke off abruptly in mid-air while Millie, building up to the voluptuous crescendo of her finale, whirled upon her pretty heel in all her wrath towards the poor, reprehensible Mac.

"Don't you have no respect for a lady, you stale, sweatin' underside of a skunk?"

Dismayed and furious, the mob descended upon the hapless trail cook and trapped within the confusion of a spontaneous melee, chairs, tables and fists flying every which way, someone inadvertently stabbed Mac in the eye with a fork. Unfortunate although this was, it did not handicap Mac in any way. In fact, Millie later maintained that the black patch lent him an air of dignity which pleased him greatly. Millie was never one to hold a grudge, and the two of them remained fast friends from the day of the Horny Toad fight until they finally arrived, inadvertently, upon the barren island expanse of Winnipolago.

Coincidentally, the webs of destiny are interwoven and tangled.

Who would have thought that after their dramatic encounter in the wilds of Montana, these two souls would find refuge from the regular hurly burly of life upon the very irregular shores of Winnipolago. But within the space of one week, the eclectic population of the island swelled by at least two with the arrival of larger-than-life Millie and noticeably less significant, Mac.

Millie's entrance was a boon to Winnipolago. Not only did her magnificent physique invigorate the male population with a fever of lust, but Millie also possessed an entrepreneurial streak that was only slightly shy of genius. She had an unabashedly commercial instinct for survival and, immediately, without so much as a carpetbag, she set herself up in business, convinced that what the islanders most urgently needed was life insurance.

Naturally, this scheme was greeted with considerable distrust, but Millie was persuasive and had a way of cornering a person both figuratively and literally, so that pretty soon they had very little choice but to see things her way. Besides, the island was small, and avoidance and concealment were futile. Millie always caught her man. Sooner or later she would catch up, and it was prudent simply to pay her in order to be able to come out of hiding.

Pretty soon that shrewd business woman had garnered most of the available spare cash, including some that had been squirreled away for decades and heavily tarnished, no longer resembled conventional currency. She began boasting about her huge commissions and, while she was enormously admired for her business acumen, few of the recently insured felt particularly comforted to know that they were now safely sheltered under the protective umbrella of Mutual Progressive of Panama.

Ironically, there was nothing very much to buy on Winnipolago, but most of the population liked the sound of a pocket of jingling coins or the reassuring feel of a clip of banknotes. But they now felt suddenly spiritually impoverished. They had kissed their green stuff goodbye, and they were dejected.

Then an extraordinary thing happened.

Millie announced to the despondent impecunious of Winnipolago that they must all march up to the church and fill out incomprehensible forms in order to get their money. These two inexplicable directives threw the islanders into the frenzy of an ant's nest jabbed and tormented with the handle of a garden rake. They dreaded that the reference to money meant that Millie had not yet finished her squeeze. Forms terrified them through a commonly shared contempt of scholastic achievement and because experience had taught them that whatever article demanded their signature also required their pocketbook. And they were perplexed at the involvement of the preacher, who possessed the uncanny predilection of stirring up long forgotten moral sensibilities and irksome regrets and who installed in the islanders a condition of melancholy that left them far worse off than before.

The bewilderment subsided within a few days when the stronger tempered denizens at last girded up their collective loins and reluctantly trudged the winding path towards the looming *tabernacle of despair* that crowned the high ground above the settlement. Millie never explained her strategy in any way that anyone could understand, but, nevertheless, she was enormously persuasive.

The Preacher had an inkstand and blotter reverently positioned upon the altar in order to lend a modicum of authority to the proceedings, which, in spite of the almost palpable apprehension on the way up the hill, quickly diminished into a hubbub of anticipation.

It was, after all, an event.

Millie struck up a lively song or two to the incongruous accompaniment of the wheezing pipe organ while one by one forms were hastily consummated by thumb-print and mark until, finally, the Preacher added his own flourish and notary stamp of bureaucratic officialdom. Health was drunk, sins forgiven and benediction bestowed, no money had changed hands and all was well once more within the excellent community of Winnipolago.

Imagine the delight, when four weeks later, the first checks started fluttering in. With astonishing regularity, Slim wheedled and coaxed his obsolete, single-engine biplane over to the mainland and in short order converted the checks into note and coin to the vexation of the bank teller who balked at the sudden run on dollar bills and quarters. Suddenly, the entire populace found themselves opulent and an air of bonhomie filled every soul with liberality and high-mindedness. It was as if the Almighty, moved by their tribulations and afflictions, imaginary or not, bestowed largess in biblical abundance upon the lost souls of Winnipolago, and all was very well.

Millie, of course, rose in both stature and personal hauteur as the indisputable Queen of the island even though the vagueness surrounding her business strategy remained unresolved until some months later.

First one, then two, followed swiftly by an avalanche of court documents, inundated the island without warning, like the Spring tides. It seems that the Preacher had signed and notarized a considerable plurality of death certificates on behalf of the population who, by all appearances, were very much alive. It was an astute strategy in any way that it was viewed except that Millie had made each one of the inhabitants their own beneficiary. It was only a small oversight, but it caused the entire enterprise to unravel like a frayed wool sweater attacked by a feisty cat.

The consternation was overpowering, and at times, it verged upon wholesale panic. It appeared to devolve into an unnerving, independent malevolence that shrouded Winnipolago in a foreboding premonition of dire consequences.

Would they have to give the money back?

But, for all the legal threats and feared ramifications, the furor eventually died down. Lulled by the passage of time and predictable forgetfulness, the episode blurred into the patchwork of reminiscence and fib that encompassed the insular psyche of Winnipolago. The money stayed upon the island, treasured up and as hidden as the secrets that possessed the souls of the populace. Millie's reputation remained intact and her esteem untarnished. Perhaps her little deception had been, after all, flawlessly crafted. Greater wisdom somewhere had shrewdly prevailed and decreed the better policy. Leaving the islanders to their own devices far out of sight and mind of civilization, in those distant reaches beyond the Northern Lights, benighted, precluded and unfathomable and not rocking the Winnipolagian boat must have seemed the best and most prudent strategy.

3.

Slim was a man of considerable discretion and very few words and, it was through those considerations and not his physical appearance, that he earned his name. Slim flew in the mail about twice monthly. But his aging aircraft was temperamental, and he had to more or less rebuild the engine after each flight. This was hardly a misfortune. Slim was considered one of the lucky ones because at least he had something to keep him occupied and occasionally, he actually left the island.

His Reverence was also fortunate. While it is true that his congregation was sparse and sporadic, prone to arrive in droves at the incident of a full-moon but otherwise conspicuously absent unless requiring a favor of the Almighty, nevertheless, the Preacher was busily engaged most of the time.

At the time of the big storm he had made a considerable profit on behalf of the Lord through a makeshift confessional whereby much of the murky, indecent conscience of the island was laid bare for a fee, on a sliding scale of course, depending on the magnitude of the infraction and the weight of the subsequent millstone.

Consequently, with this considerable largess, the Man of Cloth purchased, on God's behalf, a handsome telescope through the Sears and Roebuck catalog, in order that he might better view the magnificence and vastness of his Master's creation. The optics were splendid, alike to all God's handiwork, with a zoom capability that retrieved the finest detail and minuteness from the vast yonder, and delivered it instantaneously to his inquiring eye. Oh, the splendor! The Preacher had been spotting Millie for weeks.

When the weather was clement and a fragrant breeze

wafted from the rhythmic swell as the gentle surf caressed the shore, those of a poetic disposition would find themselves drawn to the charms of the outdoors. The sun dappled ocean and deep blue of water and sky alike, and the lazily drifting clouds that dreamed across the firmament cast a spell of mystification upon the populace.

The greater number retreated to the safety of their domiciles, suspicious of unwarranted generosity and wary of the contradictory blow that was most certainly to follow. Yet, while the majority of the islanders treated tranquility and loveliness with distrust, Millie remained the exception. She reveled in the pleasing embrace of the elements and would rush down to the beach with childish delight...

A caressing breeze wafted through her curls and nuzzled her cheek. Sea birds swooped and swirled overhead, squealing with elation. The amorous sun kissed her bare arms affectionately and gently touched her skin with balmy delight. A wave of enthusiasm suddenly carried her soul to fresh heights and all at once, throwing caution and her clothing to the wind, she dashed into the surf like an intoxicated and decidedly top-heavy nymph of nature.

There were other telescopes upon the island, although none possessed the finesse of the Sears and Roebuck model. Ravenous eyes, nonetheless, peered out from the darkness, hopeful that Daphne would stand motionless long enough for a good view because it was hell constantly to have to refocus when she dashed about all over the place.

But the Preacher possessed the Cadillac.

He could get her into his sights and hold her there while she frolicked in the waves. Caught up in the wonder of it all, an emboldening hymn might spill from his lips and stir his imagination to the heights of rapture. The mountains and valleys of the Holy Land, the cedars of Lebanon and the Pearly Gates themselves had nothing on the milk and honey of the angel of the shoreline.

As with every good thing on Winnipolago, it could not last. The folk wisdom of the island was justified. The silver lining of every cloud did indeed conceal a thunderstorm. All at once, the heavens split into shards and torrential rain descended. Poor Millie ran hither and thither in a panic, retrieving the remnants of her clothing as the discourteous wind rose and offensively snatched them again from her grasp. Trounced, she rushed away stark naked to the shelter of her cabin and hid herself under the bed until she at last regained her composure and sighed to no one in particular, "Well, I never!"

Staring at the underside of her cot, Millie was considerably chagrined and wondered if she shouldn't try to make her peace with the Almighty, and through His manifold and great mercies, at least try to get some of her clothing back. While she could think of no particular infraction that could have upset Providence in such a violent manner, she was certain of a cumulative demerit if only by virtue of being alive. She resolved, there and then, to attend a service the following Sunday and lay bare her soul to God's good graces.

And that is how the Preacher's ship came in and just as swiftly exited.

Sunday was a normal day on Winnipolago. The heavy rain had dispersed, replaced by a fine drizzle that, eventually, settled into the steady and eternal dampness that the islanders knew and loved so well. The church stood forlorn and empty, as it ordinarily did on an ordinary Sunday when no catastrophe beset the island inhabitants who could see no need for spiritual succor as long as everything remained perfectly usual.

Of course, the Preacher was always present, haunting the vestibule. Collection box in hand, he demanded the tariff before the service, lest a parishioner should conveniently neglect to pay

19

the tithe afterwards. This was pay-as-you-go commerce at its finest, ordained from On High and eminently prudent.

Millie entered, bowed. Enfolded in her ample fur-collar topcoat, proudly retained from finer and more fortunate days, and her richly colored headscarf modestly worn inside-out as a gesture of contrition, she dropped a silver dollar in the Preacher's collection box.

"Good day to you, Miss Millie!" He cackled in delightful surprise, a drip of moisture distilled upon the tip of his nose like a dewdrop.

"The service will begin whenever you are ready".

For while the Preacher always conducted the full service every Sunday, including hymns and prayers, he usually waited until late at night just in case, by an off-chance, he might snare an audience during the day. Now, overwhelmed by this comely penitent, he outdid himself. There was never such powerful oration, prayerful enthusiasm and biblical gravity as upon that dripping Sabbath. The very walls echoed with fervor and the high beams above trembled with passion as the inspired man of God banished stain, blemish and smirch from the soul of Millie and the whole-wide-world itself, for good measure.

Millie, a sensitive creature easily moved by intensity and ardor when it arose both in herself and another, swooned overcome by the good man's piety and boundless charity, and when she regained her composure, she found the Preacher at her side, clutching her to his breast, lips puckered in benediction. But it was the perpetual drip suspended from his nose that broke the spell and Millie, as worldly familiar as they come, recognized a pass when she saw one and arose in wrathful indignation.

"Get off, you silly man! I only came here to try to get my things back." And she stormed towards the door.

"And you can stop peeking at me through that darn telescope as well!" she added as an afterthought, slamming the

20

door behind her.

But for the silver dollar, the Preacher would have been inconsolable.

4.

Slim made a pickup the following week, and the islanders knew of the arrival of the mail from the backfires of the engine as the plane wove its way through the cloud cover. The little aircraft came to a bumpy landing in the meadow behind the church that had once been a cemetery before the gravestones had been recycled for building purposes. It was a far from ideal landing strip because of the numerous mounds that yet remained because they were the only means of knowing where someone was buried. As it was, flowers were often placed on the wrong grave because no one could distinguish between them.

The location of the airstrip demanded that the church double as a post office, but the Preacher would only allow the porch for those purposes, citing grave concerns about the ways of Mammon that nobody could quite comprehend. Thus, a long shelf was set into the stone wall with the various incoming letters arranged alphabetically as far as was humanly possible.

The truth be known, apart from the occasion of the life insurance scam and the subsequent lawyerly barrage, there was very little correspondence between the islanders and the outside world. But on this occasion a formal-looking envelope with an official, type-written address and an ostentatious logo had found its way into Slim's satchel. It was addressed to the Mayor of Winnipolago.

Winnipolago was without a Mayor although a few pretenders had arisen from time to time. The more sensible had been driven to distraction while the remainder had tired of official idleness and returned to their own informal inertia. But Slim possessed a systematic mind beneath his quiescent exterior and dutifully positioned the letter upon the shelf under M, with a small rock artfully placed to prevent it from being blown away.

The only dwellers of that fated isle who names began

with the letter M were Mac and Millie. Second names among the population being significantly frowned upon, the two of them might justifiably assume possession of the letter, upon that basis alone, even though neither possessed mayoral aspirations or any other claim to high office.

It was Mac, predictably, who arrived first at the improvised Post Office. He was not expecting mail being an inactive correspondent and his poor Chippewa nurse having long since departed the home of the hanging judge. She had run off before dawn after too many threats of execution from that gentleman when bourbon without water nightly, finally, had deranged him and turned his mind exclusively to his professional preponderance. *"Hang them all,"* as a constant oath became unnerving. When he himself finally succumbed to his everlasting rest, they inscribed the same epitaph upon his tombstone.

Mac had a grudge towards Slim and this occasioned his punctual arrival at the Post Office when the mail came in. Slim, well aware of Mac's animosity, flew in just before daybreak because, with his poor vision, he imagined that Mac would be unable to take a potshot at the aircraft with his old carbine, and Slim could escape detection again before being spotted. The two of them had played this game of cat and mouse across the island even since the *incident*. Slim never knew the cause of the squabble and Mac had most certainly forgotten. Nonetheless, there yet remained self-respect and principle to be upheld and Mac was the relentless servant of those virtues.

Frustrated once again, he threw down his carbine and collapsed to the ground, bemoaning his fate.

"Dang nation! Ill geet ihm ifn it tak m' hole 'ife!"

It was then, staring heavenward from that prone position and shaking his fist in order to emphasize the profundity of his oath, that he noticed the tip of the envelope protruding over the edge of the shelf above the letter M. Perplexed, he stared at the

24

strange anomaly unable quite to fathom its significance. Well aware from the force of habit that the spot belongs to himself and Millie alone, he began to deduce. The conclusion of his rumination was stubborn in its materialization, but suddenly the penny dropped and Mac realized that the tip of the envelope indeed signified the possibility of mail either for himself or his assumed beloved, Millie.

Removing the letter from the precaution of the rock, Mac stared at it, dumbfounded. He had seldom seen anything so tidily addressed and the paper was clean and unwrinkled as if the sender had required but one attempt at its composition.

Surely the missive was intended for him.

Hastily, he concealed the letter within the dark and unpleasant recesses of his long-johns and scuttled away with his good-fortune. He would lope home before the sun pierced the early sea-mist and before nosy neighbors arose from their slumbers and breakfasts, and before the pell-mell of island life should intrude upon his expeditious skedaddle. And there, in the security of his shanty, he could examine the envelope at his own convenience.

Mac had only recently made his impetuous retreat when Millie arrived at the church, having been similarly awakened by the spluttering aircraft engine in the early dawn. She had no expectation of mail either but, forever the optimist, she wended her way towards the Post Office enjoying the same quiet that Mac had similarly foretold.

The Preacher noticed her approach and eager to make amends for his impromptu indiscretion and concerned that Millie might spill the beans all over the island and thereby soil his impeccable reputation, he sidled from the shadows of the church and smiled beneficently.

"Good morning Reverend. You have no cause to worry. Your secret is safe with me but I require the return of my silver dollar."

Crestfallen, the Preacher reached into his breast pocket and retrieved the cherished keepsake. Holding the edge between finger and thumb as if it were a circle of brimstone and the testimony of all the weaknesses of his poor flesh and the sins of human kind, he dropped the piece of silver into Millie's outstretched hand and sighed an everlasting sigh.

"I hope to see you at services on the holy Sabbath, Miss Millie." He wheedled.

"Before then, if your telescope has anything to do with it," shot back Millie as she looked up to the shelf where the mail was arranged.

"Oh, Mac took your mail already, Miss Millie. He was here before dawn trying to catch up with Slim, regarding the *incident.*"

Millie's brow furrowed, and the Preacher squirmed with alarm.

"Nothing wrong I hope." He gasped apprehensively as he retreated into the depths of the impregnable sanctuary that was his refuge and where he could compose himself once more, collect his wits and reestablish his rectitude.

Millie set off at a brisk pace, single-minded resolution directing every step as her pique smoldered first into outrage and then, high dudgeon. By the time she reached the settlement, she was fuming as she careened around the cottage fences, scattering chickens and trashcans in her wake.

"Millie," Slim called. "Mac got the letter."

"I know!" She snarled.

And, one by one, the colonists called out to her as she went by, offering the same intelligence. Mac's furtive and clandestine subterfuge was known by all and sundry. The story of the official and immaculate letter was celebrated far and wide before Mac had scarcely reached his dwelling and drawn the

26

curtains. Nothing escapes the all-seeing eye of Winnipolago.

"I know you're in there!" yelled Millie. "Open the door this instant or I shall set your house on fire!"

Anywhere else, a warning, even of the vehemence of the one that Millie swore, would be greeted with derision. But upon that fair island of Winnipolago, there existed no such thing as an empty threat. Already, one or two islanders were eagerly dragging up clumps of dry marram grass, assorted sun-bleached driftwood and flammables of every diverse nature. The last occasion of comparable fun was the affair with the life insurance scam, which was described in full detail in an earlier chapter. But arson was close to every troubled heart upon the island through the decisiveness of its application. Into the pyre would go individual malice, long festering and infectious, to be lost forever in the inferno.

An energetic blaze was alike to a celebration of cleansing upon Winnipolago.

"I'm commin' owt!" cried a wretched and plaintive voice. "Don burn me 'ouse!"

Out came Mac, much chagrined, staring at the ground as he shuffled towards Millie and the crowd of expectant onlookers, the offending letter before him, unopened in outstretched hand. Millie snatched the letter, frowning at Mac in disgust.

"But it ain't even addressed to me, you old fool. M is for mayor and we don't have no Mayor."

Clearly Mac was much relieved, and a thought slowly began to percolate within his mind that not only was he out of trouble, but he might be able to keep the letter, anyway. It did not belong to anyone else.

"Well, let's open it anyhow and see what this is all about," announced Millie to the delighted crowd.

Dear Mr. Mayor:

I have been asked by the producers to enter into correspondence with you exploring the possibility of making a film upon the island of Winnipolago......

The letter was very polite and phrased as carefully as the address on the envelope was typed. The writer explained how she had searched the entire globe hoping to find a suitable island location in order to make a delightful, romantic movie... PG of course, and naturally the studio would like to hire many extras from among the citizens... who would, of course, be appropriately and generously compensated at scale-and-a-half or similarly lavish terms.

It was at this point that the assembled populace became simultaneously excited and apprehensive. The implication of acting for money inspired every heart, but the possibility of being recognized by mainlanders struck deeply.

"There'll be costumes and wigs, makeup and disguises," encouraged Millie, fully aware of their latent apprehension. "Someone'll make characters out of us and no one will be able to tell one from the other."

This lightened the mood considerably, and it was resolved, without further ado, to reply forthwith to Miss Mary Alice, in the affirmative on behalf of the Mayor, who is, unfortunately, at this time indisposed, on an extended vacation in the Galapagos.

The letter was duly composed and, through a lengthy community endeavor, signed and sealed. Mac was commanded by Millie to make up with Slim, and the two of them shook hands shamefacedly. While Slim remained entirely ignorant of the origin of the fracas, nevertheless, he took Mac's hand like a man. Letter safely bestowed in the mail satchel, Slim took off at first light. Wary through habit of Mac and his carbine, he immediately ascended into a canopy of cloud cover that all but obscured his whereabouts, were it not the incessant backfiring that interminably accompanied the aircraft.

Thereafter, there was a frequent crowd of would be movie stars loitering in the vicinity of the church, hoping to be the first to receive the glad tidings from Hollywood. Several had costumed themselves outlandishly in bizarre combinations of wardrobe borrowed from each other. They imagined that the waiting was a rehearsal opportunity not to be passed up and one that would position them in good stead for the forthcoming auditions.

In order to better tolerate the irregular intervals of languor between mail flights, the more accomplished thespians among them memorized a confusion of verse drawn from such diverse sources as Shakespeare, Karl Marx and The Old Farmer's Almanac. Many an ingénue well passed her prime discovered a latent gift and brought it to ample fruition through passionate and blood curdling reenactment of the Trojan Wars, the French Revolution, and snatches from the works of Dante Alighieri.

But the wait eventually proved unendurable and tempers began to flare. Acting was forsaken and farce steadily devolved into open hostility. Finally, the weary and disheveled antagonists beat a separate, crestfallen retreat homeward, as the better part of valor. No one cared for stardom or renown anymore and a brooding hostility arose in the collective heart of Winnipolago: *Hollywood be damned!*

Gradually things returned to the accustomed normal. Wounded pride was submerged by indifference, and bygones became indistinguishable from the many accumulated grievances that were kept battened down for safe keeping.

5.

Serenity through the absence of noise was a mixed blessing on Winnipolago. There were no cars because there were no roads and no roads because no one had anywhere to go. Additionally, the obvious geographical isolation of the island protected it from interference from the outside world apart from the periodic drops of essentials. Such was the degree of seclusion that old-timers maintained through addled logic, that the island populace comprised the global majority of Homo Erectus, the world was as flat as a plate and that Winnipolago enjoyed the distinction of being located at the epicenter, like a bullseye.

This intellectual regression was an anthropological anomaly of considerable merit and would have justified serious and extensive scientific research had scholarship shown the remotest interest. It was an example of devolution whereby mankind, under malign circumstances, steadily deteriorates to the condition of the primitive and over vast eons returns to the single-celled simplicity of primordial life. Thus, serenity as a depiction of the mentality of the Noble Savage would be recognized as a trenchant misnomer while simplemindedness strikes the nail squarely upon the head.

It would be untrue to say that there were no motor vehicles on the island. The remains of several, long since separated from their vital parts, could be discovered in peculiar locations alike to archaeological artifacts and curiosities of a bygone age of industrial precocity. Slim regularly salvaged for the remains of anything that resembled an airplane component or which might be otherwise successfully adapted. Like Sisyphus, the persistent demand of reconstruction, necessary to maintain the serviceability of his biplane, was a perpetual and monotonous destiny that eventually became accepted by him as second-nature.

While none of the aforementioned vehicles discarded

31

about the island retained their original moving parts, Winnipolago boasted one relic of considerable prestige that remained intact through its inaccessibility. One elegant, nineteen-fifty-nine, two-door, pink Cadillac remained perpetually, in all its glory, partly submerged, even at low tide, among the alluvium of South Bay.

You see, Millie had a mother and her mother once came to visit.

Millie's early stardom in Montana haunted her constantly and exacerbated her exile. She had once been a celebrity, adored by hundreds, who pursued the particulars of her standing within the world of entertainment with relish. Now she found herself a cast-off without distinction, a mere echo of her former glory. She was just another washed-up has-been: a back-number that had been read from cover to cover and thrown away.

So Millie wrote home.

"I have written to my mother!" She announced to no one in particular one morning as the island inhabitants congregated at the Post Office to check for mail.

There was little reason for her to keep this intelligence to herself because everyone already knew that she had mailed a letter and it was addressed to a lady who lived at a rural location in Montana. It was a point of honor upon the island of Winnipolago, never to keep a secret if it concerned someone else's business.

Slim, as honorary Post Master, sorted and rubber-stamped what letters there were, both on the way in and on the way out. But there was usually an additional handful of interested parties who assisted him in these operations, helping with the alphabetization and carefully adjusting the rocks that secured the mail from the occasional ocean driven flurry that, like the islanders, appeared eager to examine the correspondence.

Consequently, Millie's news was no news at all, but the anticipation of a maternal missive in reply to her own grew exponentially with each passing day. Finally, upon a fair dawn towards the end of the following week, as the seagulls squealed in unison with the cresting waves upon the seashore, and Slim's biplane spluttered down to make a clumsy landing upon the knobbly graveyard beyond the church, the dam gave way and the inhabitants rushed headlong. Oblivious to the splendid auroral spectacle that washed the pale sky with crimson and vermilion, they rushed upon the Post Office like a pack of hounds.

Passed from hand to hand and scrutinized with animal-like intuition, the dispatch was handed down the line to Millie as she entered the porch. She tore it open with a will that they all shared and scanned the contents.

"My mom's coming to visit!" she cried.

It is doubtful if any of those present remembered anything of their true mothers and it is even facetiously conceivable that there were those in the company who had the distinction of arriving in the world without any such person being involved in the business at all. But a hush of wonder had settled upon the gathering. Motherhood was an extraordinary concept in the minds of the Winnipolagians, alike to pleasant music unknown to the mind but hauntingly familiar to the soul. All at once, Millie became aware of the change. It was as if her friends and neighbors suddenly, preternaturally, appeared in a different light. Gone was the uncouth and unseemly. She found herself surrounded by a heart-rending gaggle of dejected orphans.

"My mother is a fine lady and she will want to meet you all for sure. So no swearing or cussing. Be on your best behavior and make a good impression."

Her conscience-stricken flock nodded in assent, vowing silently to mend their disorderly ways as if Mother Superior herself had commanded it.

"She will be here tomorrow," added Millie, while the

assembly gasped, awed at the momentum of events and overwhelmed with excitement.

Due to the cumbersome postal anomaly, peculiar to Winnipolago, it should not have been of any surprise that Millie's mother would be expected the following day. It was a miracle that she had not arrived already and the letter announcing her intentions, follow her a month later. But the tingle of expectation that from now on possessed the populace was palpable, and it was certainly advantageous that the wait should not be prolonged or, most certainly, something calamitous would have ensued.

The Preacher hovered at the open church door, already donned in his finest ecclesiastical attire. He resembled less the belfry bat and spider amalgamation that was his usual appearance and more a decidedly sinister Andalusian inquisitor, a remnant of centuries passed. This was a foretaste of the designs and imaginings already circulating within the Winnipolagian psyche and, once on the trajectory of extravagance, God only knew how things would eventually erupt during the next twenty-four hours.

"Millie, how may I be of serviceability to you and yours upon this auspicious occasion?" he purred.

"Hush up, smooth talker. My mother's going to stay at the rectory. And no funny business!"

The lantern jaw dropped, replaced with a mixed expression of horror and artifice. For it was true that the rectory was the finest of the island habitations, possessing both running water and an indoor privy, but the Preacher's lightening mind was already way in advance. He was intensely curious about the condition of the soul of Millie's mother and especially fervid concerning her other, more earthly attributes.

The next day was stormy, which was most assuredly taken as a spiteful omen by the islanders and did not auger well for the upcoming arrival of the Grand Dame. In justice to the weather, the people of Winnipolago considered all of its activities with

34

suspicion and this adverse swing of inclemency only served to augment an already pre-established prejudice.

Nevertheless, the truculent sea boiled furiously.

However, at last a cargo vessel was spied, pitching like a fairground shooting-gallery target, upon the distant horizon. The captain of the ship must be a man of considerable courage and determination, strong-willed and obstinate, risking the fury of the elements to deliver his precious cargo. It was a well documented fact among mainland seafarers that the reaches of Winnipolago were treacherous, only comparable in ferocity to the disposition of the island inhabitants. Old-wives-tales augmented by grim experience warned of the will-o'-the-wisp and wrecker's beacon that lured the unsuspecting to their cruel destruction. It was even speculated that a portion of the ostensibly lost maritime remnant whose vessels were destroyed upon those dangerous shores perversely remained upon the island and integrated with the population.

But storm or no storm, here was the ship cutting through the swell like a relentless javelin, spewing acrid smoke in its wake, resolute in its mission: full steam ahead.

Already various figures could be seen upon her decks, rushing hither and thither with the fear and scurry of a kettle of terrified rats. Some held ropes, alert to bind the ship fast to the harbor bollards at first opportunity, while others... But what is this? A lady with a flouncy hat of street-walker red, amidst billowing hooped petticoats and scarlet gown, flamboyant against the sober navy of the captain's livery, was beating that brave man mercilessly about the head with her parasol!

The swift approach of the steaming vessel assured its imminent arrival and within moments she was securely bound by the fore-line while the stern remained unsecured as the heavy rope sunk beneath the flood and became entangled among the refuse and jetsam that polluted the dockage.

The lady in the skirts was waving frantically while intermittently striking the captain with her parasol so that the poor man shielded his head with both his hands as he yelled exasperated orders to the terrified crew.

Millie was beside herself and her screams of excitement pierced the bedlam and furor of the deteriorating tempest. The lady of the red hat was blowing kisses towards her exiled offspring and shared the ample abundance of her enthusiasm with all and sundry. Every shore-bound soul partook of her affection as if their own long-lost parent were reaching for them and longing to enfold them in the warmth of her generous bosom.

Suddenly, an agonizing grind of metal upon metal tore through the jubilation. Cogs and gears interlocked in fierce desperation and to everyone's astonishment, the ship's davit swung in wild dementia into the turbulent bowels of the vessel and from the hold dragged a monstrous object of Solferino pink.

The ship swung wildly in the swell, its solitary lifeline taut like a noose. The boom of the crane swung menacingly under the strain of the unwieldy cargo and loomed like a gibbet over the heads of the scattering spectators below. A flash of lightening viciously rent the sky and the cargo went crashing into the shoals of West Bay.

Millie's mother seemed to blanch at the sight of her beautiful pink Cadillac plunging into the flood. It was as if the heart went out of her and even her red hat seemed to pale. She ceased her ardent gesticulations of affection towards her daughter and once more took up her cudgel and severely berated the unfortunate captain. A few horse-throated commands were heard over the commotion and all of a sudden a slicker enshrouded seaman tumbled over the beam and deftly slid down the rigid prow-line in order to release the ship from the stranglehold of its halter. No sooner had the lurching ship once

36

more regained its liberty than she bucked violently out of the treacherous harbor without so much as a fare-thee-well.

Mother and daughter blew final, solemn kisses and within moments they were lost to each other once more. The cargo vessel beat a hasty retreat, pitching and tossing in a madness of smoke and storm, until she also vanished beyond the horizon.

The forsaken sailor is his yellow slicker peered anxiously through the ocean violence but, finally, threw his hands down, dejected as all hope of escape disappeared with the retreating ship. Millie, clearly subdued but ever large-hearted, consoled the abandoned mariner in a warming embrace.

"You can stay here with us son," Millie crooned.

"We always have room for one more on Winnipolago. What shall we call you?"

She dried his eyes with her embroidered handkerchief and stared into the frightened face of a young mulatto.

"Goodluck", he moaned in piteous irony.

"Well, Goodluck, you are going to get on just fine here."

And that was how the ranks of Winnipolago were swelled by one more affable and misplaced soul, and a partially submerged 1959 Cadillac, Coupe De Ville, stark pink with dual bullet tail lights and large sharp fins, that remained similarly ensconced within the Winnipolagian, inaccessible reaches.

6.

Perhaps it was the forties or the fifties of that last century of so many astonishing, global changes, or earlier in the murky past, that pigs first arrived on Winnipolago. History and other scholarly arts become blurred over time through over attentive improvement and, in the uncertain minds of those destined to endure their three-score-and-ten upon the pastures of that fair island retreat, fact was scarcely distinguishable from fiction. Verity and yarn became progressively welded into a common and incoherent confusion of detail and, thus, a more engaging folklore replaced stark realism.

Legend has it that during a moonless watch, a lone schooner ran afoul of the rocks at Got One Point. Someone on the headland had lighted a fire and inadvertently confused the intended navigation away from the shoals and, instead, caused the vessel to run aground under the assumption that the bonfire was a harbor beacon of the mainland. Like a moth to a flame, the vessel was hurled upon the reef. Whether there were survivors among the crew remains uncertain, but a company of pigs swam through the wreckage and succeeded in reaching the safety of the headland.

Subsequent generations of swine gamboled contentedly along the drift-line in search of detritus, grunted and drooled with gratification while exhuming root and radicle, and copiously farrowed their kind 'neath wind-swept clumps of marram grass. Akin to the bipedal inhabitants, they passed their days preoccupied with rude survival and the enthusiastic satisfaction of the demands of the flesh.

The Winnipolagian, notwithstanding a conspicuous lack of scholastic and cultural acumen, endeavors to survive under primitive conditions not by preference but under a covenant with

39

destiny. There is simply nowhere else to go. For the unfortunate islanders and the pigs alike, Winnipolago is the final refuge.

That is not to say that their lives are entirely drab and without diversion or amusement. A favorite pastime of that society was horseshoes. Strictly speaking any metal object was allowed because there was only one horseshoe on the island and for good luck, it had been nailed securely to an outhouse door. The rules of the game were, consequently, flexible because of the motley assortment of projectiles and, furthermore, the overall purpose might be differently decided at any given moment.

It was a warm Winnipolagian afternoon and a pleasant, torpid contentment hung in the air. A gathering of citizens was lethargically tossing horseshoes of diverse descriptions, over the harbor wall into the sea. The loser on this occasion was whoever was unfortunate enough to hit the wall.

Mac was particularly unsuccessful at this pastime, but his companions allowed him additional leeway on account of his limited vision. Blind in one eye, his left eye performed moderately well, but he was right eye dominant and the projectiles he had gathered for the game compounded his difficulties. He adroitly hurled an old enamel saucepan over the wall, but the bucket that followed clattered noisily against the stonework.

"Mushta beecha don tod munk!"

His fellow players were astounded. Even Goodluck, new to the game and still newer to the plethora of exotic, island eccentricities that constantly confounded him, was more than usually bewildered. Mac, habitually reticent of speech through no fault of his own, was evidently piqued at losing the game. And worse was to come.

"Musta beecha to go for swine sitton."

He was proposing an entirely new pastime. That of pig riding.

Taciturn people get away with a great deal. People of few

40

words earn respect by default. No one can tell if they are smart or not but, to be on the safe side, they are treated with caution. When they do speak, their audience is caught unawares and every word appears to possess pertinence and measure.

In Mac's case, his slowness of wit and awkwardness of tongue were self-evident but, nonetheless, when he did manage a pronouncement he commanded complete attention by virtue of its scarcity.

Mac was annoyed because he kept hitting the wall with his miscellany of horseshoes. But his proposal for a pig ride was extreme. The island pigs were notoriously surly and particularly wily, having finessed complex strategies of survival and concealment that made them all but impossible to hunt. The only way to catch a pig was through the tried and trusted stick-and-boulder approach.

A conveniently large boulder is rolled up a sharp incline with the help of muscle and lever, to be precariously suspended so that the slightest disturbance would send it pitching headlong down the incline. The only hindrance to its free-fall is a short length of stick forced beneath the delicately balanced monolith with a length of string attached. A tasty bait, such as a chicken wing or a crust of bread, is secured to the string in order to lure the unwary prey to its destruction.

This established and expedient method of pig bludgeoning had evolved through considerable trial-and-error and was found to be virtually fool-proof unless some other creature should happen upon the tasty morsel and endeavor to fly or scuttle away with it.

It was unclear what Mac actually had in mind, if anything at all. But to exacerbate the situation further, the Preacher just happened to be ambling by at the moment of the outburst. His face began to cloud over like the darkening sky before a storm. His thin lips tightened and disappeared into an abrupt line. He seized a makeshift horseshoe and lurched it over the seawall with all his might. Turning upon the motley gathering, he glared at them as if one of his congregation had superstitiously removed some coinage from the offering box.

The offense was not the proposal of a pig ride, but the supposed mis-usage of the word *swine*. To His Reverence *pearls before swine* possessed sacred significance, and he was incensed that Mac's uncouth utterance might have implied a blasphemous illusion to the Good Book. All those present recognized that upon the next occasion of a church service it would be *fire and brimstone* in double measure and they silently vowed to avoid the church at all costs until the Preacher had regained his composure.

On Winnipolago, memory fades fast but pardon is hard to come by. A grudge may be harbored indefinitely like that *incident* between Mac and Slim, and no one remembers the origin. On a small island, it is prudent to maintain equitable terms with the majority. Who knows when one might need the assistance and succor of another. But aside from the survival advantages, the mutually shared predicament of exile inevitably establishes a covert bond between fellow suffers and, in any case, ostracism among the outcasts would be an unspeakably mournful misfortune.

Goodluck, with Caribbean foresight, recognized the tension and discerned the acuteness of the menace that Mac had unwittingly unleashed. He recalled the circumstances of his own heritage and knew full well of the destructive potential of unbridled rancor.

"Tha' a fine idea Mac," he yelled, in his best pidgin as if Mac had suddenly invented the internal combustion engine.

"Tha' just what we do! I tired of horseshoes. We ha' ourselves a Grand Lottery. First prize go to de one who stride that fine porker over yonder, rooting in the garbage."

Well, as soon as the Preacher saw the sport in it his

demeanor relapsed to its former status as if the sun had instantly chased all the clouds away. The fever of a gamble was balm to his soul. A smile of beneficence broke out across his face and the assemblage feared that he was going to call them to prayer, right there and then in the shade of the harbor wall.

They figured that Mac needed to be involved in the event because it was through his blunder that the trouble had erupted in the first place. And the Preacher was similarly determined to participate in the lottery. Armed with rope, Mac's old carbine and a can of kerosene, in case all else failed, they hurled themselves upon the unsuspecting porker.

The immigrant pigs of the island enjoyed an uneasy truce with the human population. Occasionally, one of their number would find itself inadvertently entrapped beneath a boulder but they never put two-and-two together nor discovered the agency whereby the accident had occurred. But this blatant attack in broad daylight was another matter entirely, and the indignant hog fought with tooth and nail against the aggressors.

It was clear that Mac and the Preacher would never catch the pig, but Goodluck, who had considerable entrepreneurial horse-sense, altered his impetuous lottery scheme and began to take bets instead. Odds were established against who would fall into the slough or be the first to grasp the pig's ear. This adjustment proved a charm, and a crowd gathered. But one should never win too easily or too obviously on Winnipolago and as Goodluck steadily accumulated significant profits, he became increasingly aware that another change of tactic was in order.

An acutely homicidal spirit had entered the sport on the beach. The Preacher was by now livid, cursing up a storm, while Mac was blue with hyperventilation and dizziness and foaming at the mouth. It was evident that they were rapidly approaching some bizarre and savage finale.

All at once, Goodluck scrambled down the beach, waving

a wad of green backs in his fist.

"You won! You won! First prize in Hog Ride Lottery!"

Well, the two of them were struck dumb and abruptly ceased their labors. The deeply offended pig squealed a final protest of defiance and sauntered off to the safety of the dunes, both to catch its wind and to try to make sense of the rude assault that had just taken place.

The various steps of logic between failing to catch the pig and winning the prize escaped both Mac and the Preacher entirely but they eagerly accepted the proffered money and thumbed through the banknotes delightedly.

With superhuman effort, the Preacher quickly reverted to his pontifical self and smiled benedictions and blessings upon the assemblage. He carefully counted his share of the spoils and retreated with purposeful dignity up-wind of the pig, to the shelter of his sanctuary.

Mac was delighted and appeared similarly confused. He took the money drooling eagerly, trying to count it as if somehow, in the addition lay the meaning of the entire episode. All at once, he looked up craftily and caught Goodluck with his good eye.

"Betten n' hoseshoes for swine!"

Goodluck eyed him back in astonishment and pondered the enigma of Mac as the old codger stumbled up the beach. Had Mac devised the entire extraordinary escapade from the outset?

7.

Scotty had resided upon the island of Winnipolago since time immemorial. For him, it was less of a hardship than for many others because, as a native of the Hebrides, he was already familiar with the Far North of the Northern Hemisphere. He had endured long winter nights with astonishing forbearance that only another kilt-wearing man could fully appreciate. There were equally unending summer days too when, finally, exhausted of the stark sunlight, a weary soul would throw himself upon his bunk and catch a short respite only to find sunrise, a few precious hours later, peering in upon him once again.

However, for any individual, the long winter isolation endured in boreal climes can be an insufferable experience. Different people respond in disparate ways towards duress, but solitude is no respecter of persons and it can strike down alike, the sinner or the saint. There is a well-documented story of a castaway marooned for an age upon a tropical island who had become so exclusively familiar with the sound of his own voice that he considered the speech of others an intrusion to his dialog and would react violently. He was eventually detained under hospital supervision for an extended season, but nothing could be done to relieve the obsessive preoccupation with his own conversation. He was finally returned to the island of his former exile. He and himself lived out their remaining years in perfect contentment.

Upon the wastes of Winnipolago, the quarantine was self inflicted. It was found prudent to endure the winter months independently because of the extraordinary conflicts that might otherwise erupt spontaneously, as the hibernal forces crush in upon the unprotected soul.

Fortunately, Winnipolagians are a resourceful bunch and the predictability of the endlessly repetitive, forthcoming condition of solitude produced a cornucopia of imaginative pastimes. The widely known astronomical interests of the Preacher and others of a similarly inquisitive disposition have already been touched upon, although their research lost some of its enticement during winter months when window curtains were tightly drawn against the penetrative northerlies.

Scotty, forever resourceful, played his bagpipes in an endless drone that could be heard the full distance from the church to the harbor, as if a sleeping bear were snoring in a cave beneath the island. Fortunately, one spring a family of mice nested in the bag and chewed relentlessly at the lining and no amount of ingenuity could repair the damage or quench the smell of rodent. Finally, Scotty threw the soiled instrument to the flames during the Mid-summer Fire Festival because St. John's Day seemed the appropriate occasion for the sacrifice.

Thereafter, Scotty sang his way through the winter months, which was a vast improvement, although, unlike his melodious ancestors of yore, his repertory was strangely limited to a few Mexican ballads. It was speculated that they reminded him of a long lost romance with a native maiden of the Central Americas because he sometimes melted into pitiable sobbing after much repetition. But in truth, he wept for his *ain tree love,* which were his pipes, and for the *bonnie banks an' by yon bonnie braes.* To sing forth in his native brogue would have broken his poor heart for sure.

"I cann dow but sigh, I canna dow but mourn," he murmured in his grief.

Upon Winnipolagian winter nights, other islanders pursued an eccentric diversity of interests but, predictably, the most peculiar diversion was the one that preoccupied Mac for interminable weeks and months. Through cunning animal instinct, Mac began his winter preparations before the cold weather locked down the island. During the heady days of late summer, he began to write. In much the same way as a squirrel gathers acorns and conceals them for leaner days, Mac detailed the clement seasons in order to last him through the impendent freeze.

Mac's survival strategy was incongruously cerebral. He compiled memory lists.

His lists were not the stuff that dreams are made up but stuff and nonsense. He captured words spilled by others as they swirled unclaimed about him and he secured them fast upon endless reams of paper, scribbled frantically lest they should escape before they were securely sequestered.

Scotty once came across a bundle of these writings during a freakish flood that presaged the late autumnal downpour with which the population was familiar and with which they had come to equitable terms. The unexpected deluge had invaded Mac's privy. It was there that his missives were conveniently stored in order that they might be readily accessible should a thought or a quotation flit by while he was occupied upon the commode.

Naturally, Scotty had endeavored to decipher the documentation, but the meaning of the scrawl completely eluded him. Mac's written word was as incomprehensible as his spoken. But he had been delighted with their return and promised an eternal friendship to Scotty that filled that Hebridean heart with dread. The event of the rescue of Mac's autography was not without consequence and it was later the following winter when an early suggestion of spring intimated its approach, that things finally came to fruition.

There is no doubt that Scotty was squarely to blame. But the hope of an end to the dreary cold conditions that gripped the island interminably inspired him with romance. His usual singing voice was modest and unobtrusive, enjoyed only by himself and his nearest neighbors. But now he threw back his head and in sonorous ecstasy, broadcast the fever of his heart to the world.

A haze of sunshine melted the frosty window panes, and they appeared as circles of luminescence like those upon a friar's lantern. A drip-dripping trickled from the ice laden roof and splashed the topmost logs of the woodpile. The old cabin creaked as the weight of winter was steadily relinquished and the sagging timbers eased off their unendurable burden.

No sooner had Scotty surrendered to the bard of spring than he knew that he was lost. Resounding melodies burst forth to the consternation of all within hearing. Dragged forth from the archives of bygone Hibernian centuries and seasoned with the exotic nostalgia of Gaelic chivalry, minstrel magic filled the frigid air as legend and rubric melded into an ecstasy of glorious optimism.

> *Awaa' wi' your witchcraft o' Beauty's alarms,*
> *The slender bit Beauty you grasp in your arms,*
> *O, gie me the lass that has acres o' charms,*
> *O, gie me the lass wi' the weel-stockit farms.*

Upon that desolate isle of Winnipolago, cooped up through an aeonian, synodic eternity comparable in austerity only to the frozen planet Pluto, a whisper of redemption lifted the heart of the old Scott and he held forth with unrestrained gusto.

> *And e'en when this Beauty your bosom hath blest*
> *The brightest o' Beauty may cloy when possess'd;*
> *But the sweet, yello darlings wi' Geordie impress'd,*
> *The langer ye hae them, the mair they're carest.*

It is true that beyond the first few verses, the lyrics, incomprehensible to all but the most stalwart of souls, wavered and a certain repetitiousness set in, but Scotty's exhumed repertoire was now limitless and there were still many weeks to come of long dark nights and scant daylight. Passion was slow to awaken in those far northern reaches, but the resounding cry of the bard shook the island people to the quick.

Suddenly, midst an ensuing verse or two lamenting, *the wander'd far by burn and brae through many a Highland glen an Lawlan*, the door was thrown open with a force of enthusiasm only matched by Scotty's own. There, bursting with delight stumbled Mac over Scotty's threshold and into his arms. Mac threw back his head and took up a seemingly appropriate chorus. There was no stopping his jubilation.

Awe mi Luve's like to a redd redd rose,
Wuts newly sprung on June:
Awe me Luve's like a melodium,
Wot switty pay'd a toon.

It sounded as if an army of cats had spontaneously decided to celebrate the equinox by murdering each other. It was all those incomprehensible scribblings that he had captured in the autumn and pored over for months and months as Mac tried to cling to happier days. It was alike to some mysterious, subterranean eruption that boiled over and consumed all in its path with determined rapture.

But Scotty and Mac's exuberant premiere sounded a chord with all Winnipolagians and from cabin and hut alike voices were raised to contribute to the general cacophony, and even the church bells began to toll with ponderous intonation.

The cold winter lost its grip and the thaw thereafter progressed in earnest. Soon icicles began to fall and rivulets of muddy water trickled along the lanes. The iron earth became spongy while the deadened, icebound harbor groaned with anticipatory freedom as the surging currents swelled and fractured the frozen pack.

Winnipolago was thereafter never the same. It became a tradition of considerable superstition and, when winter ground on with relentless harshness to the point where the Winnipolagians could take it no longer, voices would rise spontaneously in fervid contradiction and musically proclaim the inevitability of the imminent deliverance of impending spring.

8.

Eventually, Millie, consumed with boredom and thirsting for the attention that was her due, decided upon an enterprise. She opened a tavern.

The Crumpled Horn was an immediate success offering all things fishy including oysters freshly dredge from the harbor, crabs in various stages of maturity and decline, and a considerable diversity of cod that was unrecognizable as that particular fish when deeply fried and no doubt went by many another name besides.

Her ennui evaporated like a mist in the sunshine. She found herself within an element with which she was familiar and thoroughly experienced. Resembling the good days of yore, the clientele of her establishment obeyed her every whim and was exuberant upon those occasions when Millie deemed to *trip the boards* for them and show her stuff.

But Millie was not entirely happy because she remained an incorrigible romantic and upon the dull landscape of Winnipolago and among the drab inhabitants that populated that rock strewn exile there was a decided scarcity of stardust.

At this time, Joe, who was the island insomniac, was increasingly accompanied during his long nocturnal meanderings by Scotty. Their two cabins were similarly oriented towards the ocean and Scotty spied Joe many a night, lantern in hand haunting the cliff-tops and dunes and imagined that he recognized in Joe a kindred spirit of melancholy.

Scotty took to following Joe during his nighttime wanderings, and curious people began to wonder if insomnia was contagious. They foresaw an unfortunate time in the future when the entire population would nocturnally arise and traipse around in the darkness alike to a succession of zombies.

At first Scotty followed at some distance, not wishing to

intrude upon the other man's elegiac preoccupation. But eventually, a strangely loquacious man at night, Scotty could endure the separation no longer and, throwing caution recklessly to the wind, he interrupted Joe's lonely musings.

Joe was a large man in every dimension with a knotty countenance. His forehead was a blue-black confusion of swelling because, through his considerable height combined with his preoccupied disposition, he habitually struck his brow upon the lintel of his own dwelling and particularly that of The Crumpled Horn. It appeared that the tavern exerted an unusually powerful influence upon his mind which compounded his distraction.

"Mind ifn ah walk with thee, mon?" cried Scotty.

"It is a free country," growled Joe in reply, the incongruity of the statement lost upon both of them.

"Theyn ee will if'n its no trouble to thee."

Upon the rugged shoreline and craggy coast of Winnipolago would swirl and tumble the accumulated flotsam and jetsam, and bits and bobs of civilization. This was a godsend to the islanders, offering a significant distraction in which they all could share. Already mentioned is the corpse of the poor seaman and Mac's good-fortune in finding his navy-blue great-coat but there was a daily smörgåsbord of other less dramatic incidentals that eventually crowded every shelf, nook and cranny of even the humblest island habitation.

Scotty had become distracted by some uncertain object of eye-catching shape that was partly concealed within some tangled fronds of seaweed. It trapped the moon's sliver and shimmered delightfully. Stealthily, he slipped it into the commodious pocket of his parka and raced to catch up his gloomy companion.

"Ah found me a something but can no say the detail o' it."

Joe snorted morosely and Scotty vowed to cheer him if he could, but found nothing of appropriate levity within himself that might suffice. He therefore resolved upon a philosophical dialog that would surely move the mind, even if the heart was otherwise preoccupied.

"Ah am told," he began, "the' exists in that benighted country and Lordforsaken cesspit o' England, wune public house fur wune hundred mon!"

Joe stopped in his tracks, snorted once more in disgust, and again strode forward into the darksome yonder. Much encouraged at the response, Scotty scurried after his new friend and attempted another foray, drawing upon a vastly inexhaustible but dubious well of scholarship.

"Ah 'a' heard it sad, a mon cann well rememba but a million wirds but a womon 'a' no need ta. Shee makes em up as shee go along!"

With the hilarity of this last one, Scotty keeled over in paroxysms of mirth consumed by the humor of his own manufacture. He could hardly breathe, chortling and guffawing so that he did not notice that Joe had turned and stood ominously over him with a murderous look upon his moon-blanched countenance.

But by narrow fortune, Joe all of a sudden saw the playfulness of it and merely slapped Scotty with a friendly paw that nearly sent the man tumbling over into the bilge. Recovering from his imbalance and heartened by the amicable clout, Scotty resolved to pursue his advantage and once more caught up with his somber friend. Clearly, the comical approach was the most effective.

"Ye kno' the won? Hoose that ladee ee sore ya wit? That's no a ladee, that's me wife!"

But Scotty had crossed an invisible line with this last witticism and now Joe had him elevated in a giant ham-fist and the terror of it caused Scotty to shiver. But the Gods must have smiled down upon the tiresome Scott, for in the very moment when he thought all was lost, the silver-white bottle that he had found in the drift fell from his pocket and landed with a scarcely perceptible clink upon the rocky walk. It lay there in the moonlight shining like tallow and caught the eye of the towering giant.

Joe released his captive who, without another word, scampered away into the night letting bygones and insomniacs be bygone and did not stop again until he reached the safety of his modest habitation where he bolted the door fast, leaning his slight weight against it while he caught his wind.

"Ee! Thar's noo comprehendin' a mun withowt a humor!"

Meanwhile, Joe had retrieved the moonlight brimming bottle and held it to his lantern wonderingly. Something lay concealed within; tidings from some distant shore rolled into a tight scroll and bound with scarlet ribbon.

Life is curious. We imagine that we have the measure of it and that through cunning and artful reason, we may readily attain our desires and ambitions. But destiny keeps its own counsel and follows a schedule not of our making. We pursue our own initiatives and aspirations, fully expecting the anticipated rewards of our endeavors, when out of the blue we find a tightly sealed bottle of moonlight abandoned amongst the detritus. And nothing remains the same thereafter.

Joe unscrewed the metal stopper with breathtaking anticipation. He shook free the little parchment into the spreading palm of his enormous hand. Over time, countless messages had been retrieved from the drift of Winnipolago. Some long obscured through wetness and the bleaching sun, others crafted in obscure languages, indecipherable to the mean intelligence of the islander and now forever forgotten upon some dusty cellar shelf or cast headlong into a crowded attic trunk. Seldom were the contents of any particular enlightenment: *Marooned on a deserted island, longitude and latitude, such-and-such,* was very familiar and hardly elicited a nod or murmur.

But this dispatch was different. It appeared to be freshly written and new and possessed the slightest fragrance of fine perfume. Trembling, Joe pulled at the scarlet ribbon and the parchment eagerly uncurled. In the firelight of his lantern, he read the few sloping lines expectantly.

Wanted, male, at least six feet tall, handsome and of quiet disposition.
Prone to brooding along the seashore in the dead of night.

Apply at The Crumpled Horn, Winnipolago.

The Crumpled Horn was as busy and Millie was eye-catching as usual. The proprietress had just completed the final number of her repertoire and was relaxing at the bar enjoying a bowl of oysters. The denizen who managed the bar, and doubled as the waiter was Goodluck. He was frantically searching the shelving below the counter.

"I sure we had 'nother bottle, Miss Millie!"

"Well, never mind, we'll stock up with necessities at the next drop."

Millie was referring to the irregular air drop that replenished the island of foodstuffs and other indispensable supplies as a mainland, bureaucratic concession to the islanders, upon the terms that they remain where they are.

"They are sure to include ketchup."

At that moment, Joe stumbled over the threshold of the tavern having, crowned himself on the lintel once more. He scanned the room in confusion until his eyes rested upon his sweetheart. He reached his powerful arms hungrily towards

55

Millie, who appeared to melt with delight into his embrace. They cooed and purred in a transport of bliss.

"Took your time getting here, didn't you big man. I had to throw two dozen ketchup bottles into the ocean to get your attention!"

9.

Joe, at long last united in the impassioned embrace of the object of his yearning, adjusted his nocturnal ambulations to a more civilized daytime routine. He maintained that regularity, pounding along the shoreline in order to clear and invigorate his mind, but, in all likelihood, it merely assuaged the influence of the demon jealousy that always lurked about his shoulder and enjoyed provoking him during Millie's nightly musical theater.

The entertainment was wholesome, although heavily coquettish, and now that Joe and Millie were entwined as one, Joe longed for her undivided attention. Actually, his mere presence in the bar brought a measure of decorum to the place, and there were no obscene outbursts or brawls on Joe's watch. He was like a brooding bull and woe betide anyone who rattled his chain and caused umbrage to his adorable starlet.

Upon one of Joe's un-leisurely wanderings, as he belabored the winding trail to Got One Point obsessively preoccupied with the complicated enigma of his relationship with Millie, he threw a haunted glance seaward and to the cascading rocks that littered the breaking surf below. He wavered for a moment of uncertainty before rushing headlong, throwing caution to the wind, down the slippery slope to the churning sea. There, entrapped betwixt swell and reef, was a ship's life-raft and upon its platform bound in rope and sailcloth was the prostrate figure of a man.

Joe's ungainly bulk stumbled and slid fearlessly, oblivious to risk or injury as he plunged headlong to the rescue. Within minutes he was scrambling and wading between the boulders and the thrashing sea until at last he reached the raft and clambered aboard.

The trussed figure was motionless and frozen, roped fast to the raft as a spider bound its prey. His head was hidden from view in the darkness of a sail cloth poke and he was embalmed in a rag-tag slicker of canvas sheet. To all appearances, the shape was lifeless, its last breath spent and its vitality extinguished forever.

But as Joe searched attentively for any sign of a pulse and finally concluded that the man had succumbed and given up the ghost, the sprawling figured groaned. Life still remained within him and, hastily, Joe slashed the bindings with his bowie knife and hoisted the inanimate bulk over his broad shoulders and initiated his hazardous ascent up the rocky face.

Reaching the summit of Got One Point, he laid his burden down upon a bed of wind-whipped couch-grass. Carefully, he released the figure from his sailcloth cocoon and withdrew the bag from his head. The man had lost consciousness again, but it was clear that he was still breathing and there was the faintest hue of pink about the temple. The long, white shaggy beard was sea-soaked and matted and the eyes were shut fast in a criss-cross of purple creases.

Once more, Joe hoisted the limped burden over his spreading shoulders and hastily made his way down the torturous trail to the sanctuary of The Crumpled Horn. He rushed into the bar, narrowly missing the lintel but scattering bottles and glasses far and wide in a confusion of wreckage as the feet and hands of the stranger tangled with impediment and appointment alike.

Millie rushed forward in aghast apprehension while Goodluck swept away chairs and tables in order that Joe could confer his charge to the convenience of the uncluttered floor. The giant laid down his burden with tender care and gently passed a proffered cushion beneath the head of the stranger. The breathing was much stronger now and a glass of brandy tendered to his lips appeared to restore him mightily.

First one eye and then the other opened a searching slit and a hoarsely diminished voice feebly croaked to the anxious faces encircled about.

"Where am I?"

"You are safe now, Mister. You were shipwrecked on a life-raft and Joe saved your life," comforted Millie.

The enfeebled castaway searched their faces and reached a cadaverous claw towards them.

"Joe?"

"This is Joe," rejoined Millie proudly, and indicated the exhausted giant beside her.

"I owe you my life," wheezed the mariner as he collapsed insensibly into an abject heap.

"Now, you just rest and don't be bothering about things like that. We need to get you out of these wet things and into a warm bed."

She touched his lips with another shot of brandy that seemed once again to restore him mightily.

"You are an angle!" murmured the man faintly as he dissolved once more into insensible oblivion.

The Florence Nightingale in Millie became instantly brisk and businesslike, yelling orders to all and sundry alike until her patient was luxuriously ensconced in her own feather bed surrounded by a sea of pillows and cushions like some Middle Eastern pasha in a harem. His every need was anticipated and several of the other island women were happily drawn in to nurse the sufferer day and night and attend to his every whim.

At first, Joe enjoyed the status of hero and rescuer and secretly basked in Millie's increased estimation of him. But as the days followed one another in quick succession, he became aware that it was not he but the bearded patient who was now the focus of her lavish attentions.

"He is a reincarnated Avatar of vastly superior wisdom beyond the likes of mortal man," she insisted. "And we are his handmaidens."

There is an abundance of chumps on Winnipolago but the female of the species appeared to have become entirely swayed and dominated by the newly arrived and they abandoned their former good sense entirely. They crowded his bedchamber at all hours of the day and night and, alike to Nick Bottom of Shakespeare's Dream and the willing host of fairies at his attendance, they performed his every bidding.

The sea-bleached hair of the stranger, his staring eyes and droning voice seemed to exert a hypnotic influence over the women, with a magnetism as powerful as crazy glue. The females flocked to his chamber from as far away as Nutty Cove and Dead Man's Hook. It was as if Elvis Presley himself had descended among them.

Joe mournfully relapsed into his former insomnia and once more took to pacing the dunes and cliffs during the dark hours.

Scotty, who was nearly throttled and summarily dispatched by Joe but reprieved at the last second, began once more to pursue Joe upon his nocturnal rambles in baffling devotion like a faithful Highland Retriever.

"Wha ya moonin' mun. Ees plenty fish o' in the sea," heckled Scotty as he trotted after his master.

"You don't know nothin'," responded Joe glumly.

"Ee tell ye this. Ets all smook 'n mirrors. Tha man's a mesmerist. Yur shuld entirely, ta bring him ashore."

Joe abruptly checked his stride and Scotty, imagining this to be his own final moment, cowered in fearful trepidation.

"A mesmerist?" Joe repeated.

"Aye. Tha' skinny Malinky Longlesgs, he's psychologized the wommin to his will".

This was a bitter pill to swallow, but better by far than the notion that tormented Joe and wounded him to the core. He had convinced himself that the long-bearded stranger had won

Millie's heart fair and square.

"I'll throttle him!" he cursed.

"Nay, nay. No jist haud on. Ya' way too hot of a temper mun. Kep tha heid."

"What shall I do?" moaned the giant.

"Ah dinnae ken, ma heid's mince. We'll reflect whil' we dauner."

The two, hunched in silence, followed the winding path away from the settlement, passed the churchyard and on towards Got One Point. Here they stood and reflected as the night faded with the approaching dawn. As the first light bounced upon the waves and its long fingers reached towards the shore, the raft that had brought the wretched cast-away to the island trembled in the swell.

"I have it. We must get him back to the raft!" cried Joe with relish.

Scotty nodded his head sagely in agreement. This was certainly the perfect strategy, but how was it to be achieved?

They continued down towards the same stretch of beach where Scotty had found the ketchup bottle with its tantalizing message, all those many nights before. Through sheer habit and scavenger instinct, he prodded with his foot through the acrid drift-line of weed and ocean refuse.

"Whit dae ye cry thon hin? Is that noo another bowtl?"

And there in the tangle of flotsam lay another of Millie's ketchup bottles, complete with neatly rolled parchment tightly bound with scarlet ribbon. Joe snatched at the find and eagerly emptied it of its tender contents.

Gorgeous young female of mature proportions seeks strong silent man who enjoys roaming the cliffs at night.

Please contact the proprietress of The Crumpled Horn *for mutual*

61

advantage.

But, unlike upon the previous occasion when his heart had sung within his chest with delightful exuberance, on this occasion it sank like lead. Joe collapsed upon a rock, head between his hands, utterly dejected.

"Will ya noo tak' on soo," crooned the wily Scott.

"Weel repace the message with a bogie an' nun sha ken et."

Suddenly, the penny dropped and Joe sprang to his feet. Of course, they'll use Millie's message idea to rid themselves of the knavish pretender. They must fabricate a communication that will lure the scalawag back to Got One Point. The rest will be easy.

Very carefully, with bated breath, they skillfully cut away the second line using Joe's bowie knife so that now the message read simply:

Gorgeous young female of mature proportions seeks strong silent man who enjoys roaming the cliffs at night.

With equal care, they rolled and rebound the cryptic missive as it had been found but decided that they had no more use for the bottle. They could hardly contain the fever of anticipation as they wound their way from the shore towards the slumbering portal of The Crumpled Horn.

Joe was about to charge into the tavern and would have woken the whole house as his brain-pan cracked against the lintel. But Scotty restrained him with whisper finger.

"Aa ha a wey w' stealth," he hissed, and was gone before Joe could restrain him.

Scotty crept the creaking stairs like a weightless cat and soundlessly attained the sleep muted upper room. Furtively, he squeezed the latch and pried the ponderous door the width of his lithe frame and sidled across the threshold to the expansive bed. As silently as he had climbed the stairs, he surreptitiously slid the ribboned message beneath the pillow and turned to make his escape.

But at that moment, the sleeper stirred and a chorus of diminutive echoes resounded from chair and couch as the master fussed for an instant in his sleep. Within a moment Scotty found refuge beneath the bed, but by now the attendants were stirring in readiness with the dawn, to serve the capricious will of their bearded lord.

Scotty lay there for hours while the reclining despot stretched upon the pillowed eiderdown, sucking grapes and sipping nectar through a straw while the women combed his beard and anointed his scraggy limbs with perfumed oil. He rolled over, and they rubbed his knotted back and kneaded his venerable shoulders and softly crooned a melodious warble.

But all at once, one of his ministrants notice a curl of soft crimson ribbon trailing from beneath the pillow and she eagerly snatched at it, hoping for a keepsake. To her astonishment, a tiny rolled up parchment followed on its heel and the menial swiftly loosened the bow.

Gorgeous young female of mature proportions seeks strong silent man who enjoys roaming the cliffs at night.

"What have we here?" she cried as the spell of the mesmerist shattered into a thousand pieces about the room.

"The old faker's been taking us for a ride! He's just a man like any other!"

The pillowed figure suddenly realized that the game was over as their harpy cries brought a dozen women up the stairs who set upon the impostor like a flight of banshees.

In the meantime, Scotty took convenient advantage in the commotion and made a timely escape to the sanctity of his cabin.

"Ill nere comprehend tha works of tha woomin mind," he chuckled, and closed the door silently behind him.

Pillows can bring such comfort to the ailing and weary soul in a time of distress. But now, along with claw and venom, they were used in a less conventional way until the wretched mountebank was reduced to miserable disorder and painful disarray of feather and scratch. They hounded him down the stairs and harried him through the tavern door with a howling scream of feline fury. They drove his naked carcass up the winding trail beyond the church and on to Got One Point, tormenting his passage with cry and blow until at last he scrambled down the rocky promontory to the safety of his raft.

But what did he find? There stood big Joe, his broad frame barring the way. No sooner had the miserable ingrate escaped the vixen mob than he found the giant in his path and Joe was another kettle of fish entirely. With the strength of several, Joe raised the creature above his head and flung him into the swell. The howling mob and screeching gulls pierced the morning mist in jubilation while the bearded charlatan struggled to regain the raft that Joe had conveniently set afloat and which now bobbed amidst the gentle swell of the retreating current.

Without a backward glance, the castaway threw himself upon the floating platform and was swiftly carried beyond both sight and the outer banks of Winnipolago and was gone forever.

It occurred to Joe as he climbed to the headland amidst cheers of admiration, that a women's scorn, applied judiciously, was more effective than his enormous fists. And he pondered that conundrum as he climbed his way upward.

Slowly, as with the rising sun, the good women of the island wended their various ways homeward. Only one remained to receive the big man and Millie, alike to the Penelope of yore, embraced her hero eagerly and held him tightly to her rueful breast.

"I see you found another of my bottles," she purred.

10.

The correspondence with Mary Alice of Hollywood was long ago forgotten and the majority of the Islanders had found that they had successfully exorcised all acting ambitions and aspirations forever from their midst. A few retained vestigial inclinations, but nothing comparable in extent to the mayhem that had previously engulfed the island psyche. Consequently, the sudden arrival of Mary Alice herself was greeted with considerable surprise and consternation.

The significance of that isolated isle was considerably inflated in importance and consequence in the minds of the inhabitants themselves. They imagined that when they set wheels in motion with the outside world that the spinning would cease merely because they themselves had lost interest. Naturally, this self-conceited and illusory perspective did not alter actual events but merely ignored them. Consequently, while the movements of Hollywood were extraordinarily erratic, nonetheless, when the organs of commercial entertainment finally relieved themselves, they did so determinedly.

Slim carried Mary Alice in with the spreading dawn, flying above the cloud cover through force of habit, before nose diving towards the church belfry. There yet lingered a haunting suspicion in his mind that bygones may not be entirely dispersed and that Mac might rekindle his ancient and undetermined grudge towards Slim and fire a welcoming salvo at the plane, just for old time's sake.

The landing was predictably precarious and bone shaking, but:

Rain, snow, sleet or hail, we deliver what you mail !
Poor Mary Alice, unfamiliar with the resolute determination, the mystical and stalwart fiber of the servants of

67

the Mail Service in her far off Hollywood, she imagined that she had been transported to Hell. The ride had thrown all her parts into disarray and she envisioned her appearance analogous to a terrified subject of a Picasso painting.

Reeling from her ordeal, she suddenly found herself embalmed in a warm blanket with a mug of steaming coffee in her hands as the Preacher did his solicitous best to comfort and succor her. Anxious and concerned, he guided her fondly towards the vestry, where he provided her with comfortable accommodations and a welcome shot of hooch in her coffee to fortify her in advance for the trial and tribulations yet to come.

The arrival of Mary Alice was unanticipated, but, predictably, the news spread like the plague. However, through the inoculation of their antecedent outrage and disappointment, the fever of fame and fortune was no longer severely contracted and only a few die-hard thespians rekindled their former interest in dramatics.

Mary Alice was a pleasant creature, similar to a china doll in appearance, whose features had been skillfully augmented through accumulated and ongoing sculptural adjustments. Her sensual allurement was electric, as if her creators had distilled and fortified the most appealing charms of the female body while minimizing the less endearing features. She was constructed entirely without plump or beef and neither pimple nor follicle was permitted to exist at any location where it was deemed undesirable. Her wardrobe was as glamorous as her form and designed to augment her physical attractiveness into a masterpiece of agreeability and equilibrium.

Naturally, when an alien such as she, endowed with superhuman attractiveness, descends, abruptly, from the heavens and prances in all her glory before mortal man, the consequent pandemonium and hullabaloo beggars belief. The collective male consciousness dissolved into a pool of absurdity. Everyman for

68

himself, they preened, perfumed and costumed themselves in a salvage of archaic finery and threadbare menswear. Even a top-hat or two with dress-coat and tails were discerned among the motley population as if an Edwardian circus had invaded and clothed its clowns for a wedding.

Unimpressed, Mary Alice enjoyed the courteous attentions of the Preacher and remained comfortably ensconced at the rectory which she established as her business headquarters. Slim spread before her a chart of the island which revealed cove, headland and other miscellaneous locations of interest, some of which had long since eroded and shifted or become reclaimed by the ocean.

Through the isolation of the island and the alarming peculiarities of its inhabitants, visitors were infrequent and either hurriedly departed or they remained forever. But Mary Alice's visit persisted beyond the usual expectation and it was feared by the female contingent that she may never leave but instead become one of the indigenous population. The fear of such transparently inequitable competition unnerved them. But, little did they realize, Mary Alice wished to extend her stay upon Winnipolagian soil as long as possible, only to postpone the dreadful prospect of the outward flight.

Plans for the movie production were slowly shaping up but a considerable obstruction existed in its realization. Winnipolago was without a significant source of electrical power. The islanders were superstitious concerning electricity and preferred the whale-fat lantern for illumination. The only generator was an unholy monster housed in a converted pigsty behind the rectory wall. It was maintained by Slim when he was not preoccupied with the reconstruction of his flying machine and, consequently; it suffered from considerable neglect and offered only a very occasional and erratic source of current.

There was a solitary street lamp that erupted with fierce

69

light from time to time, only gradually to fade through a spectrum of diffusion, and falteringly return to its muted condition. Otherwise, the rectory alone was equipped with wiring, although the annual invasion of rodents during the winter desolation had reduced their condition to threadbare. From time to time, the Preacher, frustrated with the austerity of his exile, would tinker with the infernal generator and momentarily resurrect it to its former glory, only to watch it fade moodily, and succumb to its former repose. On these occasions, the Preacher might be seen with bloodied knuckle and oil-smeared chin, swearing and blaspheming behind gnashing teeth, face livid and contused, the image of Satan himself.

"The problem of electricity need not be an obstacle. A new generator will be shipped in with the other equipment and crew," purred Mary Alice, exquisitely.

The Preacher and Slim shared an uncomfortable stare of consternation. Clearly, Mary Alice had no concept of what a water landing entailed on Winnipolago. The last attempt had resulted in the abandonment of the 1959 pink Cadillac in West Bay.

"Miss Alice," supplicated the holy man sweetly.

"The times and tide are mighty treacherous upon the shoals of this fair land and I would earnestly advise against an aquatic assault and recommend that the supplies and equipment be delivered from the firmament."

This filled Mary Alice's soul with dread, as she was hoping that her own departure and subsequent return might be accomplished by sea. The thought of another dive-bombing flight with Slim or any other airman, and the subsequent horrendous landing in the graveyard, filled her with a dismay bordering on panic.

"But we must approach from the ocean!" she cried. "Take me down to the harbor. There must be some way to bring in a ship."

Thus, the stage was set for the finale of this Hollywood misadventure.

No sooner had the trio left the rectory than a troupe of dapper dandies appeared as if from nowhere and converged upon their wake like vultures. The unlikely procession wended its way towards the harbor, only to be intersected by a similar congregation of island women.

There was much hustling and bustling from upstage and downstage and intermingling from the wings, but within a moment the uncrowned Gypsy Queen of the island took center stage and won all their hearts with her sterling performance.

"So that's how they gussy up a manikin on the mainland!" Millie sneered magnificently.

"And what does a bumpkin like you know of the mainland?" came the practiced retort of Mary Alice.

"Prim and proper, puppet in a skirt", rejoined the Heroine rather lamely.

"The fishwife perfumed with cod-liver," countered the Hollywood lady, vacuously. But it was nevertheless true that Millie had dined on deep-fired cod for lunch that very day.

"Spangled movie harlot!" And from there on, the dialog degenerated swiftly into indecencies that would have otherwise earned the principles considerable merit for their consummate performances.

One thing led to another and Mary Alice had the appearance of a drowned rat when they pulled her out of the harbor. Although the Reverend rubbed her vigorously with a towel and fortified her from his hip-flask, the poor woman looked decidedly the worse for wear. Her exquisite proportions seemed to have fallen asunder in the brine, and her disheveled countenance lost its erstwhile appeal.

But Millie was magnanimous in victory and offered her

71

worthy opponent a measure of solace.

"Well!" she declared. "I must get myself some of that fine eau de toilette."

The Winnipolagians formed a victorious and jubilant procession onward to The Crumpled Horn where Millie, to cement her triumph, offered free drinks all round to the enthusiastic fanfare of the clientele, knowing full well that none of them were going to settle their tabs in any case.

"I am so sorry about what happened," sympathized Slim, endeavoring to comfort the wretched tragedienne.

"Never mind that!" screeched Mary Alice venomously. "Just fly me out of here, right now!"

11.

In exotic and faraway places, it is a conclusively documented fact that a full moon will inspire romance and melodramatic attachment. Winnipolago enjoys full moons aplenty. Romance and rampant promiscuity, however, is entirely seasonal. Adventure in the dead of night in the Winnipolagian hemisphere is reduced to a frantic dash to the woodpile before the stove splutters out and those caught napping are frozen into a disconcerted statue of ice.

The prospect of romance during the dismal season is analogous to a vague and troubling reminiscence of better but remote and no longer attainable days. A Utopian frolic, when the sweet fragrance of spring calls to man and woman alike to rollick and skylark, seems merely fabricated and perverse against the backdrop of a bleak and interminable mid-winter. Furthermore, inevitable destruction of the mind is ensured for those who entertain daydreaming and escapism at the expense of foresight and preparedness.

It is, therefore, hardly surprising that when the first thaw heralds the warmer weather, the entire populace of Winnipolago dashes forth like maddened lemmings to taste the joyful promise of spring and gather in bonhomie and gratitude like survivors from a terrible shipwreck.

It is the mutual endurance of the long winter months that cements the forlorn souls of that wretched outpost of civilization and discriminates them from all other peoples. They, alone, repeatedly endure the unendurable and through their tribulation partake of a common communion that forges unbreakable bonds between them.

Most Winnipolagians possess an astute radar of such an impressive potential that it would be the envy of the most intrepid explorer and mountain adventurer. It is called *the nose for spring*. In spite of inclement, sea-driven fog crawling landward, veiling and disguising, obscuring and camouflaging everything in its path with dank mystery, upon a given signal every able-bodied islander rises up as one and descends upon The Crumpled Horn.

Millie's establishment offered a refuge of varied and colorful reputation, but indispensable nonetheless to a harmonious, communal spirit. It is enjoyed inordinately and excessively by all but the most hardened ascetic who, even so, may cunningly steal a glance through the window in order to share in the festivities within, if only surreptitiously.

Before the proprietress descended upon the lonely island exile and astutely established her place of business upon those shores for the spiritual welfare of the population, the only respite from winter sufferance was the church. Initially, an apparent rivalry threatened to rock the balance between heavenly inspired authority and the gardens of Bacchus. But Millie's tacit condonation of the Preacher's astronomical interests and of his ardent passion for heavenly bodies established a workable relationship between them.

"He's seen it all already, so why mind?" was her philosophical approach and it held her in good stead with the Preacher while undoubtedly benefiting the morale of the island enormously.

As it happens, Sleazy Cove is located roughly equidistant between the church and The Crumpled Horn. The name is in no essential indicative of the disposition of the inhabitants of that region but is a colloquialism that refers to its disreputable history. Haunted by an offense of devilment in the remote and obscure past the name has endured to demonstrate to all subsequent generations the follies of larceny and fraud. Upon an island of the limited girth of Winnipolago, where one's own thoughts are shamelessly plucked without pretext and disseminated indiscriminately, treachery will not long endure before it too is

74

disclosed.

Sleazy Cove earned its name through a bet.

One dull morning in summer, when they found themselves at a loss for occupation, several companions gathered upon the cliff-tops to wager.

The first indicated an elephant seal that was frantically battling the swell.

"I'll wager," he said, "that there seal yonder struggles against the current but makes no progress at all and finally drowns."

"Naw!" replied another. "T'will gain the foreland before nightfall. I'll wager thee, my old flintlock."

"I'm with thee," chimed a third. "I'll wager thee mine own coo."

Well, they stared at the elephant seal fighting for its life until, before nightfall, it appeared to lose its strength entirely and sink beneath the waves.

"Thou art a wonder!" said one of the friends. "How did thee know such a thing?"

"Aye, a remarkable deed of skill and well worth its reward."

The honest men handed over the flintlock and the cow and retreated to their homes.

That night the wife of the man who had lost the cow asked why he had brought home no milk.

"Ah lass! I lost the cow in a wager!"

"What!" she screamed. "How'll we bide for milk?"

Reluctantly, the husband told the details of the gamble and remarked on the astonishing ability of his friend to foretell the future.

"Ye girt lummox!" she cried and proceeded to hit him about the head with a cast-iron skillet.

"I saw your fortuneteller myself this very morning tying a

rope about the tail of a seal and securing the end to a post!"

Thus, Sleazy Cove earned its resultant epithet.

At The Crumbled Horn, business was brisk. After a long and frigid winter's sojourn in the cheerless nether regions, the populace was enjoying welcome and mostly congenial company. At the bar sat the brothers Pat and Pol swathed about the head and neck with a full winter's growth of beard. Apart from their similarly whiskered countenances, they both shared a curious anomaly of speech. When flustered, they would say words backwards. It mattered little to Pat, whose name sounded very similar whether pronounced in reverse or forwards. Pol, however, consistently announced himself as Lop if he met someone on his dark walk homeward along the cliff-tops. Fortunately, everyone knew who he was even at night on account of a distinctive shuffle that he had developed over time through a confusion between his left and right. He was prone to misfitting his left boot upon his right foot, while the other he sometimes wore, visa versa.

Millie was busy behind the bar, deftly serving up plates of cod, having just performed an aria loosely based upon Puccini, to the evident delight of the audience. They were enraptured by those heaving bosoms for almost twenty-five minutes and every last man jack of them now hungered and thirsted after sustenance.

Pat and Pol appeared uncannily similar to one another in appearance and, while not identical twins, it was speculated that they shared the same parents.

"Hi fellers!" hailed Millie. "What'll it be Pat? What can I get you, Pol?"

"The name's Lop and I'll take two beers at your convenience," he replied, flustered at being addressed by Millie herself.

"And a couple for me also, if you don't mind," added Pat

with affected courtesy.

It was at that moment that an idea sprung of its own volition into the head of Millie.

"I have an idea and if you boys work with me, your beers are on the house."

The startled brothers stared vacantly at Millie and into the faces of one another, hoping that a spark of enlightenment would make itself apparent in either location.

"That is mighty generous of you, Miss Millie and we thank you very kindly," intoned the brothers in unison, understanding the free beer aspect of the conversation but completely missing the contingency.

Satisfied with their acquiescence, Millie served them their frothing beers and whispered,

"Shake your boots off both of you."

She tripped her way over to the small stage that served as the focal point of entertainment at The Crumpled Horn and clapped her hands.

"Ladies, Gentlemen and those who are uncertain where they stand, may I have your attention."

An expectant hush descended upon the crowd, every last one of them being fully alert to the perils of inattention and disregard when Millie was on the boards.

"Take a good look at these two gentlemen, Pat and Pol, seated at the bar who you all recognize and love so well. How many years have you known them? Never mind! Can you tell the one from the other?"

At this Pat's ears, scarcely visible beneath his wafting beard, became bright crimson and he tried to secrete himself into the depths of his beer. Pol, similarly at a complete loss, endeavored to fold in upon himself and become as discreet as possible. All eyes were upon them and more particularly upon their boots because Pol's tendency to mistake the left boot for the right was a notorious anomaly, even upon an island as densely populated with characters as Winnipolago.

"As you see, I have asked the gentlemen to remove their boots in order to be fair and square. I am offering two to one that the brother nearest the door is Pol, while the one at the end of the bar is Pat. Am I right or am I wrong? Put your dollar in the jar marked with a P if I am right and a dollar in the jar with the other P if you think I am wrong."

"And I will give every man a kiss who loses a dollar and the ladies will get their money back."

Money changed hands with a fluidity of an electric eel until the two jars on the counter marked P and P were full to overflowing. The clever confusion of marking the jars P and P went unnoticed by the company, and the promise of a kiss to the loser only exacerbated Millie's advantage. Pretty soon, the betting was completed and Millie clanged the ship's bell that hung suspended above the bar.

A hush descended upon the room, and a collective breath was held in anticipation.

Millie leaned towards Pat and yelled in his ear.

"And now, sir, tell me, are you Pat?"

Startled and confused, Pat regained his wits.

"Why yes, Miss Millie, I surely am Tap"

Half of the crowd went wild while the rest wondered about the kiss.

"And you sir, are you Pol?"

Pol was confused with an intensity that made him speechless until his brother had poked him in the ribs several times.

"The name's Lop Miss Millie and I thank you kindly for the beer."

But now a curious and compounded confusion descended upon The Crumpled Horn. The clientele suspected

78

that they had been gypped but could not comprehend how. Here were two brothers who, by their own testimony, possessed the names Tap and Lop, which made Millie the winner because everyone else was wrong. Therefore, Millie had won all the money.

This smacked of Sleazy Cove!

There were disgruntled murmurs and dark looks. But Millie had the measure of it.

"And now all those Gentlemen who lost their dollar and the ladies too, if they are so inclined, form an orderly line along the bar for a consolation kiss!"

Immediately, blank looks and surly mutterings dissipated like a morning mist in the sunshine and expectantly, the enthusiastic company formed an eager line and each received an affectionate peck. Thus, Millie broke the spell of winter with a clever ruse and contentedly the sleepy population of Winnipolago retreated to their cabins vowing eternal devotion to the gal who had just sold each of them a heavenly kiss for the price of a dollar.

12.

The entire day had been sultry which was a very unusual occurrence for an island situated as far north as Winnipolago and one in a corner of the ocean that was always miserably cold, and where contrary winds whipped the island from all directions at the merest whim.

The intelligentsia gathered at the bar of The Crumpled Horn speculated concerning the suffocating humidity that had descended upon the island. They suggested that it had its origin in an adjustment in the force and consequent climatic stimulus of the Gulf Stream, and that Winnipolago was becoming tropical.

"Within the next five hundred years, this island will be alike to the Caribbean with golden sandy beaches, palm trees and pineapples."

"This surely would be propitious occasion and advantageous opportunity to consider an investment in real estate."

"Our island will become the Jamaica of the north and we'll be selling piñata-coladas to the tourists, and we'll make our fortunes."

"We'll need to clean things up around here first. The wild pigs, for one, will have to go!"

"And we'll need a proper runway so that the rich swells can fly in with their private jets and then someone can start a lucrative limousine service."

"Think of all the jobs and opportunities a tropical climate is going to bring to the island."

Whether the destabilizing Gulf Stream was to blame, a tropical cyclone or the hot air swirling around the bar of The Crumpled Horn, the clammy heat was making everyone uncomfortable. Were it not for the endless flow of beer that replaced the inconvenience of the environmental anomaly with a

81

steadily increasing indifference, the otherwise kindly disposition of the population might have turned sullen.

One person was very content with the unprecedented, meteorological conditions. From the early dawn as the sun rose fiercely in a muggy sky and an ocean breeze enshrouded the island in a clammy vapor like steam from a kettle, Goodluck had been noticeably preoccupied, blissfully dreaming of his native land in the tropics. He hummed endless variations of romantic Calypso ballads to himself as he polished glasses behind the bar and stacked them neatly in a crystal pyramid.

The prettiest girl I ever saw
Was sippin' cider through a straw-a-aw.
I said 'Fair miss, I you implore
Why sip ye cider through a straw-a-aw?

All things must end and a violent thunderstorm that very night repositioned the Gulf Stream upon its accustomed course so that in the morning, the Winnipolagian climate was once again its bland and happy self.

But Goodluck was crestfallen.

"Miss Millie, I must giv' you me notice. I gotta leave"

"But Goodluck, haven't I been good to you? Don't you like The Crumpled Horn? Do you want more money?"

"No Miss Millie, it ain't de money and I like it here sure enough. But Ma'am, I'm homesick!"

"Well, there ain't no way out of here, you know that. Unless you fly out with Slim and the mail."

"Oh! no, no. I not fly wit' Slim. Saints no. I made me mine. I's goin' to build me a boat!"

To construct a seaworthy vessel is a fine art that requires considerable skill and nautical expertise. But it was not as

82

formidable a prospect as one might at first imagine. All manner of abandoned watercraft crashed and shattered upon the Winnipolagian shoals and thereby provide a bountiful source of winter firewood. Some planks and beams are conveniently shaped and often the remains of rigging and sailcloth remain handily attached so that one could imagine that a person of ingenuity might readily reassemble the miscellaneous parts and produce a fine craft fit for an ocean voyage.

Indeed, such an enterprise was attempted several times during the previous century and once within recent memory when a jumble of driftwood lashed with tarred hemp carried a seafarer as far as Pearson's Point before it was smashed to smithereens. Pearson's Point is actually named after that valiant individual who perished there. They say he had been trying to make a raft for years. But why he should wish to escape Winnipolago for the Nordic climes of his youth that were of no improvement, one cannot imagine. Perhaps he, too, was homesick.

Goodluck toiled from dawn to dusk, dragging a miscellany of drift to a convenient location where his craft might be launched. It is uncertain why he chose the harbor, because the harbor is a haven in name only. Poorly oriented, the northerlies pound this section of the coast mercilessly and no sooner is it cleared of debris for shipping than it is once again fouled and choked through the relentless interference of the ocean.

Several individuals, not otherwise, reasonably occupied, offered their enthusiastic support to Goodluck and assisted him by scavenging maritime impedimenta from the island homesteads until they had assembled numerous barnacle encrusted anchors of different caliber, a medley of colorful glass fishing floats and a box compass that unfortunately was missing the needle.

But Millie was very concerned. She knew the legend of Pearson's Point and did not want the same thing to happen to the melancholy Goodluck.

"I am worried," she announced. "Do either of you have any good ideas?"

Joe and his constant shadow Scotty stared at each other, at the ceiling and their empty beer glasses. They struggled with might and main, but no such thing as an idea was to be found anywhere.

"Yon laddie's forlorn as a numpty an' no mistakin' it," sighed Scotty.

"He don't like the island!" emphasized Joe. "He don't have no lady."

"Hmm!" puzzled Millie, and somewhere a light went on.

Goodluck was making grand progress and only lacked for a mast before his craft would be ready for its maiden and, inevitably, final voyage. He knew that in all likelihood a fine mast would be forthcoming within a few days as a stirring northerly was driving all manner of debris into the harbor.

A patient man, he set himself to painting a name on his boat.

"What you doin' Goodluck?" cooed Annabel, rhythmically. "I heard you were building a ship."

"I's paintin' a fine name, Miss Annabel," replied Goodluck, enthusiastically. "A fine ship must ha' i'self a fine name."

"Well, what's it gonna be Goodluck?" teased Annabel, tossing her curls alluringly. "Are you gonna call it *Goodluck*?"

"Oh no, sir, Miss Annabel. Dat bad luck. I must name me ship after a lady."

"Well, Mary's a mighty pretty name," tantalized Annabel coquettishly. "I knew a Mary once. She was a mighty fine lady."

"Oh no, sir Miss Annabel. There's no sense of a name like Mary. She's a bad queen who cut people's heads off!" And his eyes bulged in horror.

"Well, I don't know for sure. You are so acquainted with history!" She sucked a pink finger and cocked her head to one side. She sighed and smiled at Goodluck in unfeigned admiration. "Well, what are you gonna call it?"

What could poor Goodluck do?

"Well now, Miss Annabel, I's thinkin of a pretty name right enough."

He gazed at her, spellbound, and it seemed to him that he was melting. A strange agitation stirred and rose from the soles of his feet to his loins and on to his heart, and thereafter it stuck inconveniently in his throat.

"Goodluck, what you saying. You are so bad." She laughed like a carillon of silver bells and prettily clapped her hands to her heart.

"I's goin name dis fine ship ..." stuttered Goodluck, as he pulled himself together in desperation.

He took a deep breath.

"I's goin name dis fine ship, *The Annabel*."

"Why Goodluck! I never had a ship named after me before," she purred. "You may kiss miss if you wish."

And that is how Goodluck built himself a boat that he christened, *The Annabel*, and why it never set sail. And how Millie's best friend, Annabel, found the love of her life.

Many a patron of The Crumpled Horn marveled at the sudden change in Goodluck. His melancholy was banished as if by magic. They noticed a remarkable alteration in his disposition and caught snippets of a Calypso ballad that he sang cheerfully to himself while he poured their drinks and polished the glasses.

The prettiest girl I ever saw
Was sippin' cider through a straw-a-aw.
So cheek by cheek and jaw by jaw-by-jaw
We both sip cider through a straw-a-aw.

13.

The row started as innocuously as any other dispute, over a misunderstanding between Pat and Pol concerning the ownership of a dog. Through no fault of the hound, both brothers claimed the dog for their own because of its uncanny olfactory ability and extraordinary good nature.

There is not much wildlife on the windswept expanse of Winnipolago and, consequently, little need for a hunting dog. The pigs do not consider themselves quarry at all and resent the inference that they should be classified along with ordinary wild animals. Otherwise, there are only a few floppy-eared and seemingly perplexed rabbits that sit and stare when they are approached and, like the pigs, judge it poor form to be hunted, akin to a sort of cannibalism. The seabirds that nest in their thousands upon the face of the rocky cliffs are seldom accosted because of their oily taste. Further, they are decidedly difficult to procure, requiring that the hunter be lowered over the sheer precipice with a rope by his companions. No one quite trusts the abilities and dispositions of their Winnipolagian neighbors sufficiently enough to take the considerable risk of putting their lives faithfully in the hands of another. Consequently, the sea-fowl remain unmolested.

The reason why the dog was of such value to both Pat and Pol was because it was truffle hound.

There is but one location on Winnipolago where truffles grow during the short but optimum season and where they are safely beyond the reach of foraging pigs. A long gully stretches from the summit of the south slope of the island and meanders down towards the cliffs. Protected below the direct fury of the elements and shadowed by its own steep slopes, a grove of oak trees has become established there. The soil and moisture are perfect.

Scraggy Gorge is an island anomaly among many others and akin to the disposition of the two inhabitants of that region. The oak trees are draped with moss and lichen as the shaggy brothers are likewise generously bearded. The gnarled tree trunks with their twisted branches, resemble their rugged frames and bony limbs, and the isolation of the gully similarly suits their disposition.

Pat and Pol enjoyed a measure of independence from the rest of the community through the situation of their dwellings. Within a stone's throw from the far side of the gully was Pat's cabin, and similarly distanced from the opposite rim was Pol's little hut. They were on amicable terms with one another and had never found rhyme nor reason to fall out. Indeed, they often held a cordial conversation with one another from the front porches of their respective homes. If the wind was blowing in the right direction their exchange could be heard all over the island.

The dog was a mutual possession since its puppy-hood and, on a whim, it would wander from the cabin of one brother down the steep slope of the gully and visit with the other. This arrangement pleased all three very nicely. The dog in particular sometimes availed itself of two dinners and, while Pat would scratch it behind the ear, Pol would rub its tummy. So life was good on both banks of Scraggy Gorge, and everyone was content.

Even the discovery of truffles in the gully did not disturb the bonhomie and, when it was determined that the hound possessed an acute nose for those subterranean delicacies, the two similarly discriminating aficionados graciously shared their good fortune with one another.

The rift in this trilateral fraternal contentedness occurred one evening at The Crumpled Horn. The brothers had hailed each other across the gully and agreed to convene at the tavern in order to partake of a cool beverage. The hound was not present but had chosen to remain recumbent in a half-sleep on Pat's porch. Having crisscrossed the gully several times that day, she was tuckered out.

Consequently, it was not the dog's fault when a disagreement erupted concerning who was her rightful owner. Had she been present, it is probably safe to say that the argument would never have occurred. One look at the hound and it was quite clear that she was as devoted to both as they were devoted to her and ownership was an oblique issue that had never occurred to any of the parties.

Goodluck was at the bar and he greeted the gentleman warmly as Pat took his usual seat and Pol shuffled in moments later and assumed his.

"How is you boys dis fin' evening?" welcomed Goodluck.

"Very fine, thank you kindly, Mister Goodluck and I am sure that my brother feels the same," answered Pat courteously.

"I am indeed most well, thank you kindly, Mister Goodluck," concurred Pol. "And may we take two beers apiece if that is not too much trouble."

"Two beers apiece coming up, yesser."

Goodluck was a fine barman who was well acquainted with the sensibilities of his customers. He knew who enjoyed friendly banter, who like to remain discreet and reserved, and who was scarcely articulate. He adjusted his conversation accordingly.

While neither brother suffered from verboseness, Pat was the greater interlocutor of the two and Goodluck necessarily addressed pleasantries primarily to him. This was out of respect for the other brother, who was easily tongue-tied and no malice was even remotely intended when Goodluck turned to Pat.

"I see yo' hound stayed back home dis ev'nin' Mister Pat."

"Why yes sir, Mister Goodluck, she is plumb tuckered out asleep on my porch."

89

"You's mighty lucky wid dat hound."

"Thankee kindly, Mister Goodluck. I do not know what I would do without her," replied Pat. "She is the best dog that I have ever owned."

"A dog the finest friend a man got, surely be!" added Goodluck.

"Why yes, Mister Goodluck, that dog is my best friend in the whole world."

"Well, now, hold it if you please. She ain't your dog, she's ourn!" interjected Pol.

"Pol, I don't imply that she ain't our dog. She's just sleepin' on my porch."

But the damage was done and the strain of adversity was too much for Pol, who never disagreed with anyone, least of all his brother. He stood up abruptly and knocked his stool over, further adding to his confusion and, with eyes staring fixedly in bewilderment, he shuffled out the door.

"Pol! Pol!" called his brother. "Now what do ya' reckon has eaten him?"

The news that the brothers had fallen out spread like a wildfire across the island. The following, day a gaggle of curious inhabitants trekked up to Scraggy Gorge to see how the contrariety was shaping. To the astonishment of the crowd, they found the paths forward to the two cabins each blocked by a barricade. Upon the first was a driftwood signboard painted in bold letters.

"POL'S PROPERTY ONLY"

While the other was similarly posted with:

"PAT'S LAND AND HIS ALONE"

90

But old habits do not change abruptly and upon a pleasant evening, the two brothers might still be found occupying their barstools at The Crumpled Horn even though they had ceased to communicate directly with one another.

"How is you boys dis fin' evening?" welcomed Goodluck in his usual manner.

"Very fine, thank you kindly Mister Goodluck, but I could not tell you if my brother feels the same," answered Pat coldly.

"I am indeed most well, thank you kindly, Mister Goodluck," concurred Pol. "And may I take two beers if that is not too much trouble. I do not know what my brother wishes to drink."

"I would enjoy two beers also, thank you, Mister Goodluck, when you have finished serving the other customer at the bar."

"I will take my beers after you have served the other gentleman, if you please Mister Goodluck," contradicted Pol.

"Please tell the other customer that I do not wish to discommode him any and I can surely wait," retorted Pol.

"Mister Goodluck. I would most surely appreciate it if you would serve the other gentleman foremost, as I am in no hurry," rejoined Pat.

This interminable repartee might have continued into the night if at that moment the dog itself had not taken things into her own paws. She trotted into the bar and sidled up to Pol and licked his hand affectionately. Then she turned to Pat and plunked down at his feet and rested her head on his foot with an exasperated sigh.

"Mister Goodluck. If you do not mind, please inform my brother that I believe that neither of us owns the dog, but that the truth of it is that she owns the two of us," conceded Pat.

"And please advise my brother that I admit that he is

91

right and when you have the time, we would like two beers apiece at you convenience," added Pol.

And thus the feud of Pat and Pol over the possession of a dog was resolved by the wise creature herself, who then cemented the restored bonhomie by producing a litter of four pups of identical appearance. As the whelps grew to independence, on a whim, they might be found wandering from the cabin of one brother down the steep slope of Scraggy Gorge, to visit with the other. And this arrangement pleased all seven of them very nicely.

14.

Goodluck was not his usual ebullient self. He had somehow once more managed to descend the slippery slope of the doldrums. He remained on friendly terms with the clientele of The Crumpled Horn but as he polished glasses behind the bar and stacked them neatly in a crystal pyramid as was his normal practice; it was evident to all and sundry that something was amiss.

"Goodluck," exclaimed Millie, taking him aside, "you are not your usual self. You haven't fallen out with sweet Annabel, I hope!"

"No, no sir, Miss Millie. We's happy as two clams."

"Well, what is it then?" inquired Millie with concern. "You ain't gonna build another boat and sail away to Jamaica together I hope. You remember what happened to old Pearson!"

"No, no sir, Miss Millie. Ma seafarin' days is done for sure! Ya see, Miss Millie, is Annabel. She wont to go get us marrid!"

Millie was astounded at this disclosure and wondered at the ways of young folks. When everything is going fine, why rock the boat?

"Well, what's that girl thinking. There ain't no need for marriage on Winnipolago. No one cares one way or tother."

"I know dat fine Miss Millie but I sure love Annabel an ifn she wants a weddin dan I wants her to hav' an too. An de finist weddin you ever see. But we ain't got nothin' like dat on Winnipolago."

And thus was born in the big heart of Millie, the determination to stage the most splendid wedding that could be squeezed out of the available resources of Winnipolago and from the collective talents of the island population. She resolved then and there to apply her considerable skills of ingenuity and her notable power of persuasion to assemble all the diverse fragments of Winnipolagian culture and produce a wedding to remember.

The committee was to meet at the church in order that the nuptial celebrations of Goodluck and Annabel might at least start on the right foot. It was assumed that the Reverend Minster of Holy Orders who maintained that sacred edifice would be well acquainted with the traditional rites and rituals appropriate to a solemn matrimonial occasion. Accordingly, there gathered in the vestry a quorum of officers carefully chosen by Millie for their resemblance to normalcy.

"Ah, dear lady!" the Preacher smiled with saccharine sweetness. "And gentlemen," he added as if by afterthought. "I will now officially open this conference with a short passage from the Good Book, followed by a brief exposition of my own modest writings on the subject of the sacrament of wedlock. The section concerning marriage is drawn from my former days of service when I chaired The Ecumenical Council on Morality, Decency and Probity, upon the mainland."

There was a considerable shuffling of feet and loud coughing at this announcement, and Millie feared that the room would empty before the meeting properly started. Consequently, she forcefully stepped upon the Preacher's corns with her high-heels until that good man, head bowed in excruciating pain, howled in hasty irreverence, "I now declare this meeting open!"

"We must compile a list of all the necessary ingredients that make a fine wedding," announced Millie.

"Like a cake!" summarized Pat.

"Indeed, a fine cake!" echoed his brother.

"Therefore," continued Millie "Scotty had agreed to prepare the agenda."

"Aye, a fin bridle it will be. Whit's fur ye'll no go past ye!"

Several hours passed as the committee diligently toiled and waded through multiple layers of confusion of their own manufacture until, at last, a plausible list of the particulars of a fine wedding was dutifully assembled.

A FIN BRIDLE

KIRK
PREDIKANTER
BRIDE
BRIDEGROOM
POSEY
PARANYMPH
BEIST MON
BRIDE'S BOTTLE
BRIDE'S FLITTIN
WAYCOMING
BRIDE'S SCONE
BRIDLE CAIK
PRESENS
PYCTURE
HORS CARECHE
HONYMONETH

The committee and its officers, having fulfilled their venerable and various obligations, dispersed to consider the ramifications of the occasion of the meeting at The Crumpled Horn. But the burden of it all, of course, lay squarely upon Millie's shoulders and for once she was at a loss as to how to proceed.

"We have the church, the Preacher, the bridegroom and the bride, and we can find a best-man easily enough, although a maid will be harder to come by. Flowers we can make from paper if there are none to be gathered, but where on Winnipolagian soil are we gonna find ourselves a carriage?"

Joe looked at her like a doleful, adoring bloodhound, but he was lost for ideas. There was not a wheel to be had upon the entire island except for the four that were attached to the submerged pink Cadillac stuck in the mud and rocks of South Bay.

Joe chuckled to himself.

"I don't suppose we can get that out!" he mused absentmindedly.

"Get what, get what out, Joe?"

"I was remembering the Cadillac, that's all," replied Joe in surprise, as if awakening from a dream.

"You think we could get that thing out an' cleaned up and running? That's a great idea, Joe! Will you and the boys take care of that while I get the dresses and the cake and organize the rest?"

She pulled the big man to her arms and covered his face with kisses. What could Joe do? Naturally, he agreed to retrieve the sunken Cadillac and restore it to its former glory, although he had no idea how to set about it.

The following morning, the two residents of Scraggy Gorge received an unexpected visitor. Joe climbed the winding path and headed purposefully to Pol's cabin, which was the nearest dwelling of the two.

"Good morning to you in a most friendly manner, I say, Mister Joe," piped Pol nervously.

"Pol, I'm goin' need some help," growled Joe.

"Why... most... surely, Mister Joe," stammered Pol. "I will hail my brother!"

Pol threw back his shaggy head and yelled like a coyote.

And within moments, an answering cry sailed back to him on the landward wind.

"Well ... now, Mister Joe, if you would like to rock awhile on my porch, you surely may. My brother will be here shortly at your convenience."

Joe sat astride the stoop and waited silently for the imminent arrival of Pat. There was a rustling in the oak saplings, and then Pat appeared abruptly, shoulder firearm at the ready and pointed straight at Joe.

"I wish you a fine day, Mister Joe. But ifn you harm my brother, I will have no recourse but to open fire."

"My brother is suggestin' ifn there is any trouble, he is within his rights to discharge," summarized Pol.

Unconcerned, the giant rose from the stoop and addressed the two siblings in definite tone.

"I need to get the Cadillac outa South Bay for the wedding," he announced. "An' I need your help."

The two brothers stared at each other for what seemed to be a very long time. Their minds first of all discarded their former misapprehension that Joe's arrival spelled trouble. Then, they slowly moved onwards and lingered for a while in the vicinity of the event of the impending wedding. But the concept of retrieving the Cadillac from South Bay occupied them considerably and refused to be negotiated from any approach that they attempted.

"We surely do thank you for your visit, Mister Joe," replied Pat at last. "And we wish you a friendly good day."

"We most certainly do, Mister Joe," added Pol. "And we do sincerely thank you."

"We must slip a noose around her and pull her out with the rising tide," announced Joe, who appeared oblivious to their rebuff."

Another lengthy and uneasy silence followed.

97

"I surely predict that we will need the weight of Mac and Scotty," mused Pat, having at last found his way along the path through the practicability of his nature.

"My brother thinks that we will need both Mac and Scotty, if it is of no inconvenience," clarified Pol.

"We rope at low tide and pull at high tide," summarized Joe, as he turned and lumbered back down the steep incline.

"Well, that's a kettle of fish, right enough," mused Pat.

"Why, it certainly is a pretty kettle, and that's for sure," added his brother.

Conveniently, low tide occurred shortly after dawn the following morning as the fivesome gathered at South Bay to reconnoiter and consider their strategy. They had a considerable length of tarred anchor rope, salvaged from a profitable storm that had also generously supplied the island with abundant firewood for the forthcoming winter, in the form of deck planks and beams.

The vehicle was at least positioned right side up, which was of considerable encouragement and, in spite of the thrashing of the interminable tides, the Cadillac yet retained a semblance of its former glory, albeit windowless and severely concussed.

Joe waded into the retreating breakers with a secondary rope securely attached about his waist. The rolling surf thrashed at his barreled chest and threatened to toss him to the shoals. But the time chosen for the recovery of the automobile was well selected and a considerable proportion of it protruded through the breakers. With a deft pitch, Joe managed to capture the protruding fin of the monster and cinch the surrounding noose securely before being thrown senseless into the turbulence.

The valiant rescuers pulled against the determined outgoing tide, and through their combined exertion, they retrieved Joe from what would otherwise have been a watery

98

demise. Spluttering and choking, but otherwise undeterred, the giant struggled upright.

"We'll meet back at high-tide," he snorted, and made his way up the dunes and threw himself down upon the sand and fell into an exhausted slumber.

15.

Mac was unlucky from his anonymous birth, his abandonment to the mercy of a hanging judge and a subsequent series of events, including the fight at the Horny Toad and his ultimate arrival upon Winnipolago. His only good fortune was the discovery of the drowned seaman's greatcoat and the accompanying wallet which the ocean had, nevertheless, deceitfully snatched back from him when his back was turned. It was as if bad luck doggedly followed him like a predictable jinx.

It was, therefore, very surprising to Mac when, seated at the bar of The Crumpled Horn after his considerable exertions while wresting Joe from cruel grip of the ocean earlier that morning, that Goodluck, whose name always made him feel somehow deficient, broached a sensitive subject.

"Mac, wees been good friends, yo and me, since de day o' de pig ridin' raffle," announced his fellow conspirator.

Mac was puzzled because he did not clearly remember the pig business and he wondered if he somehow owed Goodluck some money.

"Here it ees Mac. Yous me friend an' I want you to ma bes'man at me wedding!"

Time as well as luck had dealt unfairly with Mac. While fortune had eluded him consistently, time had robbed him of much of his remaining wit and replaced it with misgiving and suspicion. The heartfelt pronouncement of Goodluck fell upon deaf ears, while apprehension flourished.

"Ee don owe ee nothin!" he declared forcefully.

"Mac, is askin' o be me bes'man on me an' Annabel's weddin'," struggled Godluck.

Somewhere, something stirred deep down, and with determined effort, it placed the thoughts and sensibilities jumbled within the soul of Mac into a reasonable condition of order. With dogged determination, it squeezed Badluck into a remote corner and received Goodluck in its stead.

"Bestman?" he queried vaguely.

"Yessa, Mac. Yous me friend an' I want you to ma bes'man at me wedding!" reiterated Goodluck.

This surprising announcement that had suddenly intruded itself into the murky labyrinth of Mac's mind was like a rustic lantern in the darkness. It did not flood the uneasy spaces there with instant illumination, but nevertheless, it glowed moderately and Mac, while uncertain of its business, enjoyed its gentle warmth.

"Bestman? You an' Annabel?" he inquired uncertainly.

"Yessa, Mac. Bes'man!" emphasized Goodluck as Mac reached for his outstretched hand and shook it fiercely.

Late afternoon, the tide was powerfully advancing up South Bay, relentlessly churning, roiling and hurling all within its path. Rock, sand and assorted debris seethed before it in a litter of foam and brine. The Cadillac trembled a little as the swell reached through the windowless carcass and worried it in a deluge of spume.

Meanwhile, the stalwart band of rescuers braced themselves determinedly at the anchor rope and waited for the count.

"One, two and *three!*" yelled Joe, as arms gripped, backs strained and muscles stretched.

Joe heaved like the Hercules of myth, completing his thirteenth labor and final penance for the prize of the love of the woman he adored.

Scotty called upon the hosts of his Hebridean forefathers and the giants of Caledonian legend. He heard within his heart the sweet drone of his beloved pipes and the cry of the bard:

"That fought and died for
Your wee bit hill and glen
And stood against him
Proud Edward's Army
And sent him homeward"

And Scotty pulled with might and main for those valiant warriors long gone to rest.

Pat and Pol, with flowing beards and wind-swept hair, appeared as matching twins of legendary Merlin invoking strange, elemental succor and fueling their determined spirits with timeless strength.

But at rope's end, Mac, with unaccustomed zeal, a transformed man, hauled with the might of Legion and with newfound resolution adjoined the common charge as the mighty men of Winnipolago dragged the rusted hulk through the chastened surf.

It was a subdued assembly that encircled the battered wreck. Clearly something extraordinary had occurred that resembled a serendipity of forces both human and consecrated. The vehicle was a shambles and lay in a contorted heap upon the sodden beach. The only portions salvageable were the four tireless wheels.

"We will build a carriage with the four wheels for posterity' sake," declared Joe, while his four undaunted companions solemnly nodded their assent.

As it progressed, the cart constructed by the intrepid five was speedily completed. In spite of their incongruous temperaments, they appeared to be possessed of a solemn resolve. While the newly born vehicle closely resembled a hay wagon, aggrandized with twin bullet tail lights, the extemporaneous decoration merely added an aspect of romance to the conveyance. The difficulty lay with the tires. The rubber had been torn to shreds and dissolved to pulp in the ocean's fury and the naked wheels grated coarsely upon the shingle pathways in a most aggravating manner. The solution lay in the tarred anchor rope, which was expeditiously reapplied and bound to resemble a tire. Soon a sturdy, albeit awkward, conveyance was assembled fit for rustic royalty.

A bond of profound significance had become established between the Heroes of the Elements as they forgathered in solemn unity upon the occasion of the prenuptial festivities. Evidently, much preparation had simultaneously ensued, whereby floral arrangements and comely decorations adorned the hall of The Crumpled Horn.

"I am so proud of you men!" sighed Millie. "This is a grand day for those sweethearts. You must be mighty pleased to be chosen as the godparents of the happy couple."

It had not occurred to those stalwart few who had assembled for the prenuptial celebrations that their commitment was to be lifelong but the consequence of the occasion was magnificently emphasized by Pol, who could not resist a retort.

"We is mighty proud also, Miss Millie. And I would like to request two beers apiece for my brother and myself and two more for our each of our companions."

A chorus of cheers arose from the assembly as everyman felt himself included and an evening of conviviality ensued irrespective of who was friends with whom.

16.

The best man awoke full of trepidation. He knew that the forthcoming and auspicious occasion required that he be very much alert and faithfully responsible. After all, he now had an extended family of loved-ones to consider, none of whom he could remember being related to before. But he was determined and resolved to do his level best to live up to Goodluck's profusion of friendship.

But old habits die hard and entangle the motley soul unawares. Mac could scarcely comprehend where he was to be and for what purpose.

It was at that moment that a soft tapping announced the opening of his humble front door.

"I surely do hope that I do not discommode thee in any way Mister Mac, but I thought it my solemn duty to request a moment of visitation on account of your sterling heroism with the Cadillac."

Who was this vision of loveliness who had entered the Hades of the soul of Mac and shone her fair and virtuous comeliness upon his threshold.

"Ee canno say," stumbled Mac. "Are you com for me destruction?"

"No, silly! I am the maid o' honor. My name is Divinity."

A storm gathered threateningly within the crook of Mac's fervid imagination and he wondered if it would engulf the whole of Winnipolago as it had many times before, and smash all that lay before it to ruin. But a gentle hand assuaged his fears and a tender voice assured him of her comfort. He raised his troubled head and the little lantern within his reclusive soul that his friend Goodluck had kindled brightened suddenly.

"Ee will go with you to the weddin," he announced. "An tak' your hand gladly."

Weddings have, since time immemorial, suffered from the elements of unpredictability that perversely intrude upon those occasions of solemnity and reveal who is decidedly who, and who is not, as they claim. And so it was upon the occasion of Goodluck and Annabel's wedding.

Everything that was humanly possible to arrange was thoroughly devised and prepared. But a contrary element doggedly intruded, as if determined to disrupt the occasion.

"Do you take this man to be your awful dreaded husband?" was only further exacerbated by, "Now, may I kiss the bride?"

The Preacher himself, that stalwart servant of the most High, was the guilty offender.

But Millie kept a tight rein on the proceedings and concealed the several indiscretions and awkwardnesses of the Bible-Thumper with loud coughing and copious emotion. Thus, the wedding proceeded with benevolence and amity until the blissfully happy couple exited the church only to be showered with rice, whereupon, as if by cue, an unkindness of ravens descended and nonchalantly devoured the entire confetti.

Notwithstanding, the nuptially-entwined gracefully retired to the porch where the marital chariot awaited their service. Comely as it was, it elicited an excitement betwixt bride and groom only shadowed by the memory of the interminably harping sermon of the Preacher.

"Well now, Goodluck!" piped Annabel, "we are off to a fine start, indeed!"

"Yes sir, surely! De'es here is good omen for sure, Misses Annabel Goodluck."

Unfortunately, the astute and detailed planning of Scotty had inadvertently neglected to include a system of conveyance for the carriage and it refused to move of its own volition. It was at that moment that Divinity whispered discretely into the ear of Mac:

"Surely Darlin' thou canst save the day!"

Suddenly a lone figure raced to the shafts and tugged as if his back were to break, but the stubborn conveyance would not budge.

"I surely feel," murmured Pat, "we could lend a helping hand to ourn brother Mac."

"This was my attitude entirely. A helping hand would be most generous."

And the brothers pushed and heaved with all the strength they could muster.

Joe, ashamed for an instant that he had not sprung to the assistance of the newlyweds at the first sign of impediment, applied his colossal bulk to the task, only to be augmented by the frail Scotty. Between the collective determination of the several, the chariot spun its wheels with delight and sailed from the churchyard with precipitous inevitability towards the shoals of South Bay.

Calamity strikes once in a while, but when it consistently rears its formidable head, mankind is justly permitted to question its intent. Is fallible humankind truly to blame, or do the Gods play at dice with the diverse destinies of mortals? This question is posed rhetorically for those that fail to see the greater picture.

Suddenly, the tumbling chariot veered of its own volition and came to rest at the threshold of The Crumpled Horn. The deranged duo, newly wed and bemused after a befuddlement of priestly and automotive calamities, assumed that the ordeal of the willful carriage was merely a feature of the festivities.

When they were finally gathered, all of a chortle, charmed and blissful, it only remained for the speeches in order to complete the auspicious evening.

Glasses were raised in portentous moment. The bestman

was hailed to the rostrum.

"Pray silence for the bestman," someone intoned.

Mac stumbled ungraciously towards center stage. He fumbled bewildered and confused, wondering where he was, until a sweet and angelic stage-voice whispered:

"Thou canst do it, Honey!" And therewith, Mac spilled forth a torrent of articulation.

"We dragged da car from the waves for dis couple, an we'll toil exceedingly everafta fur da happiness."

The assemblage, fortified through free sustenance, roared to the rooftops, while quietly, the eyes of Millie and Goodluck met for a moment. There was a pause, suddenly broken by the sweet voice of Annabel Goodluck.

"This here is the finest weddin' I ever had!" And she flung herself upon Goodluck and enfolded him in her embraces.

17.

While all good things are moderated with time, they are nonetheless soon replaced by additional adventures. And so it was upon the fair island of Winnipolago. No sooner was a modicum of normalcy achieved when something else unexpectedly reared its head and challenged the population to the quick. Winnipolagians prefer a mundane existence that requires only economical effort, but that was not to last even upon that remote outpost of civilization where the inhabitants existed without significant outside interference.

Trouble suddenly descended upon Winnipolago in the form of a hot-air balloon containing a duo of aeronautic zealots who had sailed the contraption all the way from Italy with the intention of circumnavigating the globe.

Their landing was spectacular. An easterly gale had whipped up a vicious squall that unexpectedly dumped a monsoon of drenching precipitation upon the island and, just as abruptly, it was gone once more. The flooding was surprising, but not especially severe. Winnipolago was familiar with climatological deviations and soon a warm sunshine broke through the cloud cover and dried the sodden lanes and fields.

But the squall had delivered something far more unexpected than a mere outburst of rain. There, entangled among the stunted oaks of Scraggy Gorge, hung a monstrous, multicolored balloon from which dangled a severely deranged basket containing two screaming Italian aeronauts.

The contents of the basket had tumbled into the gully below while the two men clung to the edge of the wickerwork and a precarious branch that stretched out over the chasm.

Pat and Pol had simultaneously witnessed the erratic descent of the craft from their respective porches and, in alarm, had hailed one another across the gully as soon as the squall abated. Now they hurried to the scene of the crash and to the assistance of the wildly gesticulating Italians.

"Aiuto! Portaci giù da qui!" they yelled. "Una scaletta, una scaletta!"

"I am very sorry to advise you two gentlemen," called Pat. "But we do not comprehend your language."

"My brother wishes to remark that we do not understand," added Pol.

"A ladda eh! Bring-a a ladda to gett-a down-a," called one of the fliers to the bewildered brothers. "Capire?"

"We regret to inform you gentlemen that we do not possess a ladder of sufficient length, but we may find you a stout rope," explained Pat.

"In other words, we'll return with a rope very promptly," elaborated Pol.

"Che cosa stanno dicendo?"

"Non lo so."

"What-a you-a saying-a?"

But the brothers had retreated to their respective cabins in order to cobble together sufficient rope to get the two men down from their perch in the swaying branches. The oak trees that extended down the steep slope of the gully were of modest stature, nevertheless, the descent was going to be difficult because of the treacherous incline. Fortunately, Pat and Pol were abundantly familiar with every trail and winding footpath and they soon returned with a coil of spliced rope of varying dimension and gauge.

From the basket, one of the Italians lowered down a length of cord that dangled from the deflated balloon and to which the brothers then tied their own of heavier caliber. Steadily, and with considerable trepidation, they pulled upon the cord and drew the cable into the nest of branches.

"Now, Gentlemen, if you please," instructed Pat. "Pass

the rope over the branch and we will lower you down one at a time."

"My brother wishes to explain," added Pol, predictably, "that we will lower you to safety at your convenience."

"Overa the brancha?"

"Correct," confirmed Pat. "Over the branch."

"At your convenience, of course," intoned his brother.

The Italians looped the rope over the stout branch on which their basket and themselves were uncertainly suspended. The brothers wound their end about an oaken limb and, as the first of the men clung to the other end, they were able to achieve a controlled descent and bring him safely to earth.

"Thankayou! Thankayou!" exclaimed the first. "Youa sava our lifa."

"Me brotha wisha to thankayou for a savin' our lifa," reiterated the other as he, too, reached the ground.

"You are most surely welcome," replied Pat courteously. "We are pleased that you are safe."

"My brother wishes you to know that he is very glad," added Pol.

"Cana youa take us to the telephono?" asked the first. "We calla the Embassy."

"Me brudder wisha to make a telephono to the Embassy."

Just at that moment, the old truffle hound meandered up the gully followed by a string of puppies.

"Guardare il bel cane!" cried the airman. "Beautifula doga!"

"Si, il bel cane!" agreed the other. "My brotha lika your doga!"

The first scratched the hound behind the ear while the other rubbed its tummy.

The hound, for no apparent reason, sidled up to the first

111

Italian and licked his hand affectionately. Then she turned to the other and plunked down at his feet and rested her head on his shoe.

Pat and Pol stared first at the animal, then at the airmen, and then blankly at each other.

Finally, Pat seemed to awaken as if from a spell.

"We don't got no telephone on Winnipolago," he explained. "But we can take you to The Crumpled Horn."

"My brother wishes to add that The Crumpled Horn is a tavern," explained Pol. "Ifn you would like, that is."

"Una taverna! Si. Per favore!"

"Me brudder wisha to visita the taverna," added the other. "A vostro piacimento."

The patrons of The Crumpled Horn were unaware of the descent and destruction of the hot-air balloon because of the abrupt fierceness of the squall that had driven everyone to cover. Therefore, they were enormously surprised when the foursome straggled into the bar.

"We found these gentlemen at Scraggy Gorge and they require some assistance," announced Pat.

"They arrived in a balloon," added Pol, at a loss to elaborate.

"Yous mighty welcome fa sure," hailed Goodluck. "We ha bot food and drin!"

"Thankayou! Thankayou!" exclaimed the first Italian. "We lika due birre a persona."

"Me brudder wisha two birre eacha!" added the second. "Ata youra conveniencia."

Rumors spread thick and fast that Pat and Pol had rescued two Italian travelers from certain death and that the two strangers were noticeably handsome in the manner of the

Mediterranean. With puzzling elaboration it was mysteriously intimated that the aeronauts possessed an uncanny resemblance to Pat and Pol although they did not correspond to any physical feature.

Soon the entire population had rotated through The Crumpled Horn in order to view the strangers. Millie had made them welcome in her typically effusive manner.

"Whata una bella donna!" flirted the first.

"Si. Lei è una bella donna!" agreed the brother. "Beautiful lady!"

They kissed her hand gallantly with affected politeness and were it not for a threatening growl from Joe, who knows where it would have ended.

It was explained to the two travelers that there was no exit from Winnipolago except if they wished to brave the skies in Slim's old biplane. But the brothers were adamant. They each feared parting from the other, and it was out of the question that they would escape separately. Writing a letter was similarly impractical because of the unpredictable nature of correspondence with the mainland.

"We musta menda tha balloona!" announced the first.

"Si, we menda tha balloona!" agreed the other. "Ifa youa donta minda."

Eager to share in the fun, the islanders agreed to assist the aeronauts in whatsoever way they could. The ladies eagerly promised to apply their sewing skills to patch the balloon, while the men agreed to repair the basket and attend to the rope work. But the immediate task was to untangle the damaged airship from the clutches of the oak grove and remove it to a safer location.

The combined ingenuity of the islanders, as was demonstrated by the salvage of the Cadillac, could be formidable. And upon this occasion, the men wished to see the handsome

113

Italians on their way as much as the women desired them to remain. Consequently, work proceeded at a fast clip up at Scraggy Gorge, but the sewing was attended to in a noticeably lackadaisical fashion. Fortunately, the several sail-makers among the male population were able to take up the slack when the women floundered.

But the Italians did not merely compensate the Winnipolagian exiles by their good-looks but also added enormously to the cuisine of The Crumpled Horn. Both brothers were excellent cooks, and the menu expanded from suspicious slaps of deep-fried cod to an array of Italian specialties that sounded like verses from an opera.

Cod Parmigiana
Fettuccine Alfredo with Cod
Linguine with Clam Sauce and Cod
Squid and Cod Marsala
Shrimp and Cod Fra Diavolo
Spaghetti with Tomato Sauce and Cod

Pat and Pol, the truffle hound and the puppies, all became much attached to the Italian aviators and often they would descend into Scraggy Gorge and search for truffles together.

"Ina oura country we also hunta truffels buta we tama piga," explained GianPiero.

"We tama the Italiano piga to finda the truffle," added Giuseppe.

"We ourselves possess many fine pigs," replied Pat. "But they are mighty ornery!"

"The pigs are disagreeable creatures," added Pol. "They may only be caught with the rock and stick method."

"Rocka anda sticka?" inquired GianPiero. "Whata isa

thisa?"

"Me brudder wisha to knowa thisa rocka anda sticka," elaborated Giuseppe.

Thus, the finer points of pig hunting were discussed in detail as well as the comparative merits of the Italian *maiale* against the Winnipolagian ill-tempered beast of a decidedly mean-spirited nature. But the days wore on and the balloon was nearing completion. Most of the belongings of the aviators were successfully salvaged from the gully except for the radio that was damaged beyond repair. It was this broken keepsake that GianPiero and Giuseppe presented to Pat and Pol as a memento of their friendship and, in return, they received a bag of the choicest truffles.

The morning of the launch arrived. The giant balloon was carefully unfurled and rapidly inflated by the burner flame and a clement sea-breeze. The entire population assisted in the operation and, as the balloon swelled with hot air, she began to lift until GianPiero and Giuseppe raised their arms as a signal and the Winnipolagians released the ropes. There was never such a waving of handkerchiefs and a blowing of kisses, and many an unhappy tear was shed.

Pat and Pol waved their final goodbyes as the balloon soared high into the cloud-cover and out of sight. Sadly, they returned to Scraggy Gorge and settled upon their respective porches as the dogs wended their way down the gully first to one brother and then to the other in a vain attempt to cheer them up.

Some weeks passed, and things were returning to normal on Winnipolago when Pat and Pol settled upon Pol's deck after an early morning truffle scavenge. As they sat, taking in the early morning sun as it warmed their faces, they heard a faint crackling sound.

"I can make no sense of that sound," announced Pat. "What can it be?"

"I too have not heard of it before," replied Pol. "Although I think it comes from within my cabin."

The two pushed open the front door and peered into the shadows. The sound was coming from the broken radio!

"Pata, Pola! Wea doa nota knowa ifa you hera."

"Pata ana Pola! Me brudder wisha you a heara usa."

"Wea arriva homa safa!"

"Ma brudder wisha to thanka for the truffles!"

18.

Beautiful Divinity enjoyed a singular reputation upon Winnipolago as a reader of tarot cards. Although the future held little hope of the grand adventures of fame and fortune and the area of love was decidedly limited in scope, nevertheless an eager following relied upon her services on a regular basis. They enjoyed the tantalizing pictographic representation of their lives as juggler, charioteer or emperor. The lovers, the magician and the hanging man all possessed singular significance, offering timely warning concerning romance, good fortune or sound advice on who to avoid while the Fates were contrary.

Predictably, the Preacher took exception to Divinity's skills but remained confused at the threefold contradiction of her striking appearance, the theological association of her name and her uncanny ability to be correct in her augury. Surreptitiously, he sometimes availed himself of her skills and admired her charms lustfully during the reading.

Divinity's attraction to Mac was not entirely founded upon their mutual participation in the wedding party, but he had sprung to her notice through a curious incident of presentiment, provoked while preparing a cod dinner. This spontaneous event of ichthyomancy was not a particularly unusual event for Divinity who, although she preferred the tarot, similarly presaged events through an examination of a plume of smoke, the shapes of clouds and, of course, tea-leaves.

The difference upon this occasion was the sudden and unexpected occurrence of it.

The fish was fresh from the trap and had been moments before thrashing wildly in a bucket, hoping to jump the rim and regain its freedom. Fishing was a significant industry on Winnipolago, occasionally conducted with rod and net from the rocky bluffs, but usually, and more conveniently, sea life was captured and held in a corral that took advantage of the incoming and receding tides to isolate them. All manner of sea creatures were penned in this way and most of the fish went by the generic name of cod, irrespective of its species.

Divinity had taken the living fish from the bucket and was about to remove its head and gut when it turned to her pathetically and she noticed that it was blind in one eye. She caught her breath in astonishment and immediately an image of Mac sprung to her mind and she saw him walking the drift-line in lonely isolation.

In an instant, she returned the fish to the bucket and carried it down to the water's edge in order to return it to the ocean. To her astonishment, as she released the creature to the elements and straightened to make her way homeward, she glimpsed the stooped figure of Mac in the distance, walking the lonely beach.

"I surely do not comprehend this strange clairvoyance," she murmured to herself. "What can be the meaning of this?"

Mac was curiously moved by the several events surrounding the wedding that significantly imposed themselves upon his former complacent isolation. But the entrance of Divinity into his solitude was the most remarkable. The exchange between the two, prior to the wedding when Divinity had come tap-tapping at his door, was not merely social. You see, Mac had experienced a troubling dream.

Dreams are inevitably incoherent and do not explain themselves in the conventional manner of ordinary speech. Instead, they address themselves to the recipient metaphorically and figuratively. In his bifurcated and astonishing dream, Mac found himself standing on the shore while a boat containing numerous passengers was steadily rowing through the surf away from the beach. There was an early morning mist that hovered over the waves, but the sky was brightening towards the horizon.

Mac felt that he had been left behind and he was deeply saddened.

The second aspect of the vision was extremely mysterious. He was idly swimming in the shoals about the cliffs to no particular purpose and without objective or ambition. Suddenly, he found himself trapped behind a trellis of wicker and there was no escape. He struggled and floundered, but could not get away. All at once, a hand reached down through the water and gripped him by the neck and threw him on the land. There, to his astonishment, he flapped and struggled like a suffocating fish, worse off than when he had been in the trap. Then an extraordinary thing occurred. As if by enchantment, gentle arms lifted him and released him back into the brine and a kindly voice called after him:

"Swim away, thou art safe now."

Mystified, Mac awoke with the profound impression that he had narrowly escaped certain destruction.

When Divinity entered his cabin she was shocked by the bundles of papers that littered the shelves and the accumulated stacks that were piled against the walls. This was Mac's entire summer scribblings complied throughout his long sojourn of countless years on Winnipolago.

"Why! Mister Mac! I had no idea thou wert a writer!" she cried in astonishment.

At that moment, a strange remembrance arose at the sound of her voice and hovered in the soul of Mac and vividly his dream returned to him. And in his confusion, he blurted out:

"Are you com for me destruction?"

This enigmatic outburst took Divinity by surprise, but

119

with a little coaxing she was able to learn the salient details of Mac's dream.

"This is most timely, Mister Mac, because I have my tarot cards here before me in this basket. If thou wilt, I will read the particulars of your destiny."

According to custom, Mac shuffled the colorful cards and returned them to Divinity, who laid them out in the form of a wheel.

"Mac, I read most immediately, The Wheel of Fortune, The Hanged Man, The Fool, and many a watery sign. And I see Twins and The Hierophant. Honey, through misfortune, thou hast missed the boat thy whole life and become a fool! Thou art a fish out of water whose real calling is The Hierophant."

At this point Mac repeated the unfamiliar hyponym, but in the interest of avoiding levity at this very profound moment, his rendition of the word will not be transcribed.

"A Hierophant was a person who interpreted mysteries in olden days. But the twins Mac, that's me and thou! Honey thou art my twin! And thou art a Hierophant too. But with you it takes the form of poetry!"

And she waved her arm towards his piles of summertime composition that littered his home.

Thus, it was that a poet was born to the island of Winnipolago. With concerted effort and much encouragement from Divinity, Mac's writing became increasingly articulate. His new stature was steadily recognized, and it was suggested that he send a volume of his collected works to the mainland.

It was with great excitement that Slim charged into The Crumpled Horn one evening, waving a newspaper about his head like a banner.

"He done it! He done it! Mac's poem is in the mainland newspaper!"

Slim was pressed from all sides, but it was Millie who was handed the newspaper. She cleared her throat and read Mac's poem to the assembled Winnipolagians.

Mild moments of reflection rouse the drowsy soul from summer's trance.
The windswept headland tells poignantly of bleak winter's approaching grip
And Winnipolago stirs from long and blissful sun-drenched days.
Wary of icebound darkness and endless solitude, we gather winter fuel.

Poem by Winnipolago Mac.

19.

The isolation of Winnipolago was historically assured through the abruptly changeable character of the weather. The barometer might rise or fall dramatically without notice and invite calamities of untold dimension in its wake. Additionally, the sheer cliffs and rocky shoals that defended most of the island dissuaded even the most intrepid explorer from the direct assault and seafarers were obliged to negotiate the treacherously unpredictable harbor at their peril.

Through otherwise long since forgotten centuries there lingered the stuff of legend that earned Winnipolago another ominous reputation. There arose from the former days of the oak-hulled sailing ship, a misgiving that the island inhabitants had intentionally positioned bonfire beacons about the headland of Got One Point. It was maliciously assumed that this was done in order to confuse unwary mariners into imagining that they were fast approaching the benign inlet of the Mainland estuary, while in reality, they were moments away from imminent destruction upon the perfidious headland.

While it is true that numerous fires were indeed ignited about the cliffs, they were never malevolently intended but inflamed merely to celebrate the mid-summer Fire Festival of St. John's Day. It is conceivable that, inadvertently, some deranged soul, maddened by the austerity of an interminable winter, may have escaped the refuge of cabin and hovel and unwittingly kindled a modest fire to keep himself warm. But to call Winnipolago an island of merciless wreckers would be a gross and unkind overstatement.

Time passes swiftly and things change accordingly with surprising rapidity. Through the onslaught of technical invention, the insular condition of Winnipolago was no longer assured its former privacy and covertness. The advent of radar and of the ocean jet-boat, that could readily negotiate its shallow waters, dashed its impregnable status to smithereens and made certain that intrusion was inevitable. It was only a matter of time.

It was late in the morning during a fine spring respite from the severities of winter that the craft was first noticed. There lay, at anchor, within the shoals of South Bay a boat of garish red and black with sleek lines similar in appearance to the unfortunate Cadillac in her prime.

It was Joe who first spotted her in the bay as he wended his solitary path through the dunes. Startled, he wondered at the streamlined and strident appearance and marveled at how it had managed to cross the treacherous shoals. There did not appear to be any occupants, and it was as if the craft were deserted. He approached with caution and hailed the jet-boat:

"Ahoy! What do ya want?"

But there was no reply and his voice echoed dully about the rocky cliffs of the bay. The preening sea birds looked about startled but promptly returned to their own concerns, indifferent to the perplexing affairs of men.

Joe trudged his way through the dunes towards the Crumbled Horn. He was deeply lost in thought and apprehension, unable to fathom the strange arrival of the deserted jet-boat.

"Where were the men who piloted the craft so skillfully through the barrier rocks and more significantly, what did they want on Winnipolago?"

The Crumbled Horn was steadily awakening from a raucous evening of dance and jubilation. Convinced of the banishment of the frozen winter, the population had made merry the previous evening and well into the night, only to return to the comfort of the beds with the approaching dawn. Goodluck was diligently clearing the debris of the festivities and restoring the furnishings to their usual upright condition.

" Mister Joe! How is you dis fin' mornin?" welcomed Goodluck in his usual manner.

"Goodluck. We got a problem. Where's Millie?"

"Why Mister Joe. Miss Millie 's upstairs. She be don shortly I wager," answered the perplexed barman.

Joe swiftly ascended the stairs and strode into Millie's bedchamber.

"Why my soul, handsome. You are in a hurry to see me! I'm just puttin' on my face."

"Millie," replied Joe with a concerned look as he wove a huge paw around her waist. "There may be trouble. We have strangers on the island!"

Joe relayed the events to Millie as he had experienced them, and apprehensively expressed the reason of his concern.

"It's some kind of fancy boat that can cross over into the shoals and there is no one aboard."

"They must be somewhere out there in the dunes," mused Millie uneasily.

While, of itself, the arrival of an unfamiliar vessel was of no particular concern and the many benign reasons for its sudden appearance within Winnipolagian waters might easily be explained. Nonetheless, the peculiar condition of the craft and its capacity to broach the natural fortifications of the island without notice was worrisome.

Suddenly there was a volley of loud and angry voices from the bar and Joe plunged below in three swift strides.

"Now hold it there big boy. Just you take it steady now and no one will get hurt!" yelled a savage voice at Joe's turbulent entrance.

Below in the bar stood three wild-eyed and dangerous men. About their waists were strapped menacing handguns while one of them wielded a savagely curving boat hook that he held against the pulsing throat of Goodluck.

"We don't have to concern ourselves with the big fella. He's just a dumb bear with no brain!" sneered one of their number. "Now lay down on the floor and stay still or the Negra loses his windpipe!"

It is fruitless to repeat the typical repartee between thug and hostage that has been reiterated so many times before in written works of fiction and thoroughly popularized with tedious predictability in film. Therefore, we will merely summarize the events as follows:

Basically, Millie came downstairs and advised her beloved giant to stay still upon the floor. The licentious thugs, naturally, baited her with suggestive innuendo with which she was thoroughly familiar and remained not in the least bit impressed, although she disliked the lack of courtesy and respectfulness.

Some menacing growls emitted from the wooden floor where Joe lay but he prudently remained where he was. Goodluck was released and was thrown to the floor, where he nursed his bruised neck and torso. And, as the dust settled, the principle malfeasant got to the point and amidst threat of murderous retribution for noncompliance, demanded to know where the treasure was.

Only astonished and empty looks greeted the criminals. The three islanders stared in disbelief and wondered if perhaps Mary Alice had, after all, organized a further reconnaissance to Winnipolago and these three were merely actors. But the uncouth mannerisms and obviously violent ways of the villains dispelled this idea almost as fast as it was formed.

It was unsurprising that no amount of, "Why fellars, you got the wrong idea!" or "Are you crazy or something?" could dislodge the obsession of the criminal mind that was convinced that the hostages were merely concealing the truth. A characteristic of the malefactor is that he or she imagines that every other person thinks and behaves in the same manner as themselves. Consequently, in their eyes, the Winnipolagians were obviously reticent to hand over the booty and must be persuaded through violence.

"Now, hold on there, you boys!" ordered Millie. "What makes you think that there is a hidden treasure on Winnipolago?"

"This!" shouted the ringleader as he unfurled a newspaper and stabbed a stubby finger at the script.

"The Treasure of Winnipolago!"

Millie took the newspaper and immediately her eye fell upon the footnote.

Poem by Winnipolago Mac.

"You boys are a bunch of jackasses," Millie derided them. "This here is a poem about the beauties of the island written by our local rhymer."

"I never met such clowns in all my life!" she added.

This appeared to take the wind out of their sails before they once more resumed their insistent menace and threats, although with subdued conviction.

"Listen, you loggerheads," yelled Millie. "I'll read it to you as it is supposed to be recited and you'll see how you misconstrued the whole thing."

Oh, raging torrent below the steep that awakens treasures of the deep.
Neath mountain tower and rocky scrag, how could mere man this treasure drag.
Concealed by Ages long forgotten, cursed wealth, ill begotten,
Shattered timber, beam and spar, thrashed to splinters upon the bar.

The wrecker's art of guile and worse, voiced again in homely verse.
Lest we forget our shady past, and strive to make amends at last
Who knows what cruel thing then arises careless of treasure's many guises
And as they trample in disregard we finely receive our just reward.
To harm another by any measure, denies the heart of its true treasure.

Millie delivered the poem with stunning eloquence, intoning every word and syllable with grace and ease. Goodluck was moved almost to tears while Joe turned his head away towards the wall. Her delivery was exquisite and left no shadow of doubt in the minds of the criminals that they had made an enormous mistake.

Once again, to avoid further tedious cliché we will omit the predictable dialog between the thugs and the three innocents gathered in the bar. To save face, they swore desperate warnings and threats and promised to return at a later date to pillage and despoil should it appear that there was an island treasure after all.

This last menace disconcerted Millie considerably, and she recalled Joe's earlier warning:

It's some kind of fancy boat that can cross over into the shoals.

And she realized that the island was no longer impregnable.

But Millie need not have worried because the Gods had taken a kindly liking to the unusual souls of Winnipolago and they were moved at the common plight of the islanders and their remarkable courage. They now determined to intervene.

Unbeknownst to the threesome, who returned to their craft as it lay peacefully at anchor in the rocking surf of South Bay, the inlet at this time of year, when the water was clear and

128

becoming more inviting after the cold winter, was populated with hosts of jellyfish who arrived there by the smack, for purposes of reproduction. Why the wretched men did not discover this interesting phenomenon is difficult to comprehend, but violent individuals frequently sacrifice measured reason to their passions. Had they noticed the jellyfish and considered the implication of such a vast host upon the mechanism of their craft, they might yet be around to discuss the matter.

Hot with humiliation, they sprang into the jet-boat and raised the anchor. Within moments, the engine burst into furious life and the craft flew across the waters of South Bay and out upon the open ocean. But now an extraordinary thing occurred. A compound of miscellaneous species of jellyfish was drawn into the jet unit with disastrous results. Unable to control the vessel at high speed while the engine was gorged with mutilated jellyfish, the jet-boat spun out of control. It careened over the crashing waves and was instantly demolished into splinters upon Pearson's Point.

Thus, the adventure came to an abrupt end and the extraordinary incident of the treacherous treasure seekers who mistreated the good-hearted companions at The Crumpled Horn was gratefully laid to rest. Neither trace nor remnant was ever found of the three thugs. It was thought to rename Pearson's Point, *Three Thug Point,* but Millie insisted that it remain as it is.

"Pearson was a good man, and it remains a fitting tribute to him," she explained. "We don't want to be reminded of those others!"

And that more or less is the end of this Winnipolagian tale except for one discreet detail. Mac was naturally proud that yet another of his poems had been published in the newspaper, but he was also strangely disquieted at the distress that it had inadvertently wrought. He seemed withdrawn for many days until, one night, Divinity spied him as she drew her curtains for the night. He was making for Got One Point with a lantern shining before him and a shovel over his arm.

Quietly, she wrapped herself in her night-robe and stealthily followed Mac up the trail. To her astonishment, Mac was descending the treacherous path down towards the breakers. Some distance above the surf, he began to dig and pry vigorously with the shovel until he suddenly loosened an avalanche of rock and debris that tumbled down the slope with an almighty rolling crash and concealed the remainder of the path entirely with an immense inundation.

Apparently satisfied with his labor, he regained the cliff top and looked at the destruction below.

"Now none'll ever find the treasure!" he murmured. And he made his way homeward.

"Thy secret's safe with me, old man!" whispered Divinity as she followed discretely after his retreating shadow.

20.

The June solstice, or St. John's eve, was celebrated enthusiastically upon Winnipolago. It is unknown why this festive occasion should loom so large in the sentiment of the islanders, but, nevertheless; it remained a tradition of considerable significance. It was an occasion when several otherwise neglected observances were combined that may otherwise have remained completely lost to insular posterity. Thus, St. John and St. Nicholas shared the event with the maypole while the traditional bread, cheese and beer of St. John's was augmented with Christmas pudding.

Every islander participated according to their own particular inclination.

The Preacher ostensibly frowned upon pagan rituals and had it not been for the beer, the cheese and widespread bonhomie, he may well have excommunicated himself for the duration of the holiday. But, ever a man of flexible principles, he threw himself wholeheartedly into the proceedings and organized a beauty contest.

Pat and Pol, reticent and retiring, took it upon themselves to erect the maypole in the cemetery and decorated it skillfully with tarred rope appropriately ribboned to add a variation of color to the June, May-dance.

"I am certain our contribution will be a considerable success," declared Pat.

"I concur wholeheartedly and further, I agree with your sentiment," added Pol.

Naturally Divinity offered her fortune-telling services while Mac, situated at a folding table beside her, furnished those predisposed with a skillfully crafted poem *in the very moment of inspiration* and inscribed upon parchment for their own personal possession.

Upon a makeshift stage established for the purpose, Scotty offered ballad and sonnet in inexhaustible enthusiasm from his reservoir of Hebridean and Caledonian strains.

> *You've had a cruel mither, Willie,*
> *And I have had anither;*
> *But we shall sleep in Clyde's watercraft*
> *Like sister an like brither.*

Millie and her entourage at The Crumpled Horn catered the entire affair. Joe hauled tables and chairs to the cemetery on the wedding chariot and set up a trestle for the many and varied foodstuffs, including Cod Parmigiana, Fettuccine Alfredo with Cod, Squid and Cod Marsala and a huge keg of beer.

The only one without an occupation was Slim, whose expertise lay in rebuilding the engine of his biplane and braving the elements in order to deliver the mail. He suggested that he could offer rides like a barnstormer, something that he had always yearned to do. But that idea was greeted with an emphatic refusal. However, Millie, ever resourceful, had another idea and set Slim the task of removing the various parts of the Cadillac that might operate as lighting and to endeavor to bring the generator to life, at least for the evening.

Everything was going according to plan. The Preacher's efforts yielded many a smile as the beauties of Winnipolago briefly commandeered Scotty's stage for the judging. At first the Preacher assumed that judgment, as a man of the cloth, was his own exclusive prerogative, but the crowd and the ladies themselves prevailed and, unanimously, estimated their own beauties as very nice indeed, giving the bemused Preacher a peck on the cheek for his trouble.

The maypole was a great success, and the islanders danced in confused circles of entanglement about it, uncertain of the essential rhythm that is required for its skillful execution. This excited the truffle puppies to delirium, and they too ran and skipped, tugging every loose strand with obvious delight and turmoil.

Thus, fortunes were told, poems read and sonnets were sung, all to the mutual delight of the Winnipolagian population. The feast was broached with combined enthusiasm, and it looked as if nothing could eclipse the pleasure of the festivities. But as the revelry ensued, while dancing and laughing echoed through the still evening air, something very unexpected came into view. An enormous multi-colored balloon approached the island from the ocean and steadily descended upon the knoll directly above The Crumble Horn.

Gusts of warm air wafted over the assembled revelers as the aeronauts deflated the bag and descended gracefully among the gaping and delighted population below.

"Pata, Pola! Everya body. Wea coma back toa Winnipolago!" cried Giuseppe. "Ifa youa donta minda."

"Ma brudda 's appy to see youa ana wisha to thanka for the truffles!"

Nothing more remains to be said. The challenge to the crestfallen men folk of the island quickly dissipated as the festivities once more roared into life and during the ensuing feast, it was discovered that the aeronauts both possessed wives and children of their own in Italy. And they promised that the next time they visited, they would bring their families along.

Suddenly, because an end remains strangely incomplete without an encore, a frightful, spluttering and coughing was heard from somewhere behind the church. The old generator had sprung into life at the hand of Slim and a medley of little lights, including the bullet lights from the pink Cadillac burst into a delightful star-shape of color at the top of the maypole, unfortunately only to wane abruptly moments later. But it was a fitting finale to the celebrations and the signal to kindle the St. John's bonfire of driftwood and accumulated rubbish, constructed intentionally as far away as possible from infamous Got One Point. Thereby, with a little luck, Winnipolago might yet remain insignificant to the outside world for many years to come.

* * *

EVERYTHING BITES, SCRATCHES AND STINGS
A Thousand Days in the West African Bush

This utterly authentic and exciting memoir is presented without embellishment. Between 1971 and 1974, English born Julian Hamer traveled for three years in West Africa, catching and exporting reptiles and amphibians back to Europe. This involved living in the bush sometimes far from civilization and for months at a time. During the course of these extraordinary adventures, he and his colleague, Karl Bischof, an Austrian, experienced Africa at a time when many new countries had only recently come into being after a long colonial history. The cultures of the many peoples as well as the fauna are beautifully and intimately described through a direct experience of life in the bush lived as the rural Africans themselves experienced it.